SWEET SEDUCTION

Allie Jordan

A KISMET™ Romance

METEOR PUBLISHING CORPORATION
Bensalem, Pennsylvania

For Bob Knight, a very special angel who was Will and Libby's first friend. Thanks, Bob, *Sweet Seduction* is as much yours as mine.

ALLIE JORDAN

Allie Jordan is as southern as moonlight and magnolias. After thirty-five years of marriage and eighteen romance novels, she still believes in the fantasy of romance. When Allie isn't writing, she's enjoying her three grandchildren, visiting antique flea markets with her husband, or teaching creative writing.

Other KISMET books by Allie Jordan:

No. 41 *SPIDER'S WEB*

ONE

"I look like a boy!" Libby Spencer stood in front of the floor-length bathroom mirror inspecting her nude figure self-consciously. "A twenty-seven-year-old boy!"

With a sigh of disgust, she threw her head back and raked pale-pink fingernails through the chignon she wore during her working hours as assistant manager of the Peachtree National Bank. The movement left her soft, brown hair tousled and loose around her face.

Better, she decided, but it would take more than that to make Will really look at her. She needed help and she intended to find it. Libby took a deep breath and began to read the directions from the book anchored open by a box of bath powder on the bathroom vanity.

Angel Harper's *Secrets to a More Exciting Sex Life* guaranteed to light a fire in the dullest relationship. Libby fingered the narrow box that was to be the instrument of the first lesson. She ran her hands up and down, crossed her arms nervously, and glanced back in the bedroom, hoping there was enough time to carry out her plan before Will came home.

Peering intently into the mirror once more, she took another deep breath and began. Twenty minutes later she turned and faced her reflection with pink-cheeked embarrassment. She wasn't sure any longer that this was such a good idea. Even *Cosmopolitan* magazine poked fun at Angel Harper's cutesy approach to attracting your lover's attention. But Libby was no bold woman of the nineties. And Will was definitely the kind of man Angel's instructions were intended to reach: completely unaware of the fact that he was taking Libby for granted.

The transparent plastic food wrap she'd covered her body with had distorted her dark-peaked nipples and the fluff of fawn-colored hair below, turning her into a curiously childlike creature, rather than the sensual being Angel Harper's directions had promised.

With a worried frown, Libby wondered if Angel's suggestion to give the man in her life an early Christmas present by meeting him at the door, stark naked and wrapped up in see-through plastic, would arouse him as promised, or make him burst out laughing. If Will was in his usual unperceptive frame of mind, he would probably walk right past her and never notice. Being in love with an absent-minded genius was frustrating.

The plastic wrap stuck to itself as advertised and Libby was glad she'd only covered the middle of her body. The most difficult part of the wrap had been the arms. She'd secured one, then she'd thrown the roll over her shoulder and wound herself up in the plastic to cover the other. At least she could still walk, she thought, and decided to scout the living room for an appropriate display area for her surprise. She took a deep breath, reached for the doorknob, and prayed that Will hadn't come in without her hearing him.

"Damn!" She'd wound her hands up in the sticky material. She tried to grasp the knob through the plastic. But the more she reached, the more wrapped she became.

"Double damn!" Libby fumed. It had taken her nearly half an hour to wrap herself in the first place. Now, if she took it off, she'd never get it right in time. And taking it off looked more and more impossible by the minute. What was she to do? If she had Angel Harper here right now she'd cheerfully wrap her—halo, book, and all—in plastic and stuff them in the furnace.

Libby shook her head in sheer frustration. Her impulsive plan to shock Will into a frenzy of desire was beginning to seem more foolish than sensuous. And to make matters worse, Libby began to sweat inside her airtight cocoon.

As perspiration trickled down her body, Libby squirmed uncomfortably. Now her nose began to itch. She scrunched her chin down and tried desperately to scratch the itch with her shoulder. It wouldn't reach. Finally, she gave up and in sheer frustration began counting the squares in the ceramic tile.

Two hundred sixteen tiles later, she changed to

singing Christmas carols. Where was he? Surely this wouldn't be one of those nights he got involved in some project and forgot to come home. After two choruses of "Jingle Bells" and one of "Here Comes Santa Claus," she decided she'd welcome Rudolph the Red Nosed Reindeer, if he'd open the door.

By the time Libby heard the sound of the door handle being tested, she regretted ever having seen *Secrets to a More Exciting Sex Life* by Angel Harper. If she and Will ever found time to put up a Christmas tree this year, she was determined to use a star instead of an angel on top.

"Libby, are you in there?"

"Yes!" Libby screamed out in relief.

"Is there something wrong? Are you sick?"

"No. Yes. I mean, no." The elation she'd felt at hearing Will's voice turned first to anger, then dismay, and she couldn't hold back her embarrassment. "Oh, Will, I can't get out. I'm stuck.

The door rattled fiercely for a moment before springing open with a vengeance, allowing Will's lanky body to come crashing through. His look of concern changed to bewilderment and he contemplated Libby, a flesh-colored lump of cellophane crouched in embarrassed frustration on the toilet.

"I don't know what you're doing, Libby, but it looks awfully uncomfortable. No wonder you couldn't get the door open." Will shook his head, turned away, and began to unbutton the corduroy shirt he was wearing. He draped it over the schefflera tree, unzipped his jeans and stepped out of them, leaving them where they lay as he pulled on faded blue sweatpants. "Is dinner ready?"

"Dinner? No!" Libby snapped. It wasn't working out at all like she'd planned. Will wasn't supposed to be hungry; he was supposed to be aroused. "No, dinner isn't ready. I've been . . ." she took a deep breath, trying to hold back the tide of tears threatening to close off her throat completely.

Modern women of the nineties don't cry, she told herself. They meet an awkward situation and handle it. But Libby wasn't terribly modern, not when it came to Will. "I've been tied up," was all she could manage.

"Bad day at Peachtree National, huh? What are you doing, anyway?" Will was sitting casually on the end of the bed, exchanging the loafers he'd been wearing for tennis shoes.

"I'm . . . dieting," Libby said defensively, a dare in her voice that did little more than cause Will to look at her for a moment before reaching down to tie his shoe laces. "This is what they call a body wrap. The wrap makes you sweat off the inches."

At least that much was true; she was certainly sweating. Libby jerked her arm desperately, trying to tear a corner or loosen the wrap so she could free herself.

"But, Libby, are you sure you need to diet? You look okay to me." Will leaned down, picked up the jeans and flung them over the chair.

After three years of marriage, Will was so accustomed to her that he probably wouldn't notice if she weighed two hundred pounds and had sprouted warts.

"I think I'll take a short run while you get dinner;

to take the edge off my appetite. I must have forgotten lunch again.''

Libby stared with unbelieving eyes. He was actually going to walk out and leave her like this. *At least I know how your stomach feels,* Libby wanted to scream.

''Will Spencer, don't you dare go out that door. Don't you understand, I can't!''

Will stopped and turned back to her, a puzzled look on his face. ''Can't what? Cook? So, we'll call for pizza. You know I don't care what I eat.''

''No, that's not what I mean. I can't get out of this . . . this stuff. And don't you laugh at me, Will, I'm warning you,'' she sputtered. ''Just get the scissors and cut it off.''

''Well, I'll have to admit, that's an interesting concept, but it seems to me that there must be an easier way to diet.'' Will opened the bedside table and took out a pair of silver-handled scissors. ''Can you move? I think I could work better in here.''

Libby stood gingerly and walked in short geisha-girl steps into the bedroom, trying not to see Will's head-shaking expression. He circled her slowly, examining her as though she was a perplexing piece of art work that he couldn't quite figure out. Finally, he asked in amusement, ''How do I get it off?''

''How should I know, Will? I had a hard enough time putting it on.'' She heard her voice quivering. ''Just clip.''

''Guess you did. Maybe, the next time you think you need to diet, you would consider doing a little running with me. It would sure work a lot better than some fad like this.''

Will managed to clip away the upper two-thirds of the plastic. He pushed her back on the bed and began tugging gently at the bottom section. The embarrassment of the moment slipped away as her body began to respond to his touch. Will slid his hand beneath the plastic and tried unsuccessfully to pry it away from the fawn thatch of hair below.

"I think I may have to give you a haircut, honey," Will said with a hint of glee in his voice. "I don't guess you intended to, but you seem to have created something of a chastity belt here."

"I might as well be wearing one," she said under her breath. "To be perfectly truthful, Will, this isn't a diet, anyway. It was supposed to excite you, only I got it wrapped all wrong and then I couldn't get out of the bathroom and . . . Ouch!"

Will paused in his hair cutting and looked at Libby, knowledge dawning slowly in his eyes. He flexed his fingers absently beneath the plastic wrap for a moment before he clipped away the last strand of plastic, replaced the scissors in the drawer and said, "Uh huh."

Libby felt a tremor start at the base of her neck and run down her spine and she looked up, sure that Will shared her thoughts, until she saw the laughter in his eyes.

"Libby, where in the world did you get such a crazy idea? Have you been taking some kind of weird new women's sex class with that flaky friend of yours, Dixie Kendall?"

"No, I haven't," Libby protested angrily. It was obvious that what Will was thinking was definitely not what she had in mind. She rolled dejectedly away to the other side of the bed. "And don't call Dixie weird. She's my oldest friend. She just likes to be different."

"Odd would be a better word." Will seemed oblivious to Libby's shattered ego. He was lumping her seduction plan in his mind with Dixie, and Libby knew that was the end of Angel Harper's chapter one seduction scene. She was almost glad when the phone rang and Will reached for the receiver. She sat up, lips clenched tightly, holding back a threatening dam of protest, as she heard Will agree with the caller.

"Sure, I was about to take a run anyway. I'll stop by and maybe between the two of us we can figure it out."

Well, that answered her earlier question. He was actually going to leave her to jog over to help somebody solve some problem. It was too much. Libby jumped to her feet, plowed past him and into the bathroom, slamming the door. She heard the door swing slowly open behind her. Will's forced entry had destroyed the lock. She couldn't even throw a proper fit, she fumed. Ready to scream in desperation, she began to count.

"One, two . . ."

"Libby, are you all right?"

"Three, four . . ."

"I'm going to stop by Pat's shop and help him take one of those faulty pacemakers apart . . . okay?"

"Five, six . . ."

"If we can spot the problem, maybe we'll be able

to move up Fred Hughes's surgery at least two weeks.''

"Seven, eight . . .''

"You don't mind, do you? You seem to have . . .''

"Nine, ten . . .'' Her counting trailed off as she took in another gulp of air, let it out slowly, and forced herself to answer quietly.

"Of course not. Dr. Will Spencer couldn't refuse to help build a machine that will save poor Fred Hughes's heart.'' Under her breath she added, "It's only my heart you ignore.''

"Libby, what's wrong?''

"Go ahead, Will. The wrap was a dumb thing to do. I'm very tired. Please go on. I know how important your work is.''

She'd like to ask him more about what he was doing. But her mind just didn't understand mechanical things, and the few times he'd tried to explain, she'd felt like a dummy when she didn't have any idea what he was talking about. Soon, she quit asking about his work and quit talking about hers.

Will didn't intend to neglect her. Back when he was building homemade telescopes, she was what he had needed: a cheering section and an appreciative audience. But now he had associates who cheered and hospital boards as audiences. Somewhere along the way, she'd been replaced in Will's life, and little by little she'd filled her own needs with her job and the people she helped. She didn't know how it happened, but they seemed to be striding along parallel lines; together, but not touching.

Still, she was proud of Will. She appreciated his dedication. After all, she approached her work at the bank the same way. But with a bank you could lock the door at a reasonable hour and go home. She couldn't complain because Will was so involved in his work; it was so important. Every improvement he made in the tiny computers he designed was immediately incorporated in the medical equipment the university was researching. His reputation was no longer confined to Atlanta, Georgia. He was becoming internationally known.

"Well, if you're sure you don't need me . . ." Will stood behind her, studying her curiously, still the unknowing, innocent genius she'd loved for over half her life. He didn't have the wildest idea what she was talking about.

Underneath her growing frustration, Libby felt ashamed. Will loved her and he really didn't intend to cause her such grief. She truly wasn't jealous of his work. She was jealous of his time, and the mind that ran round a problem until it was solved, excluding everything else. She'd known from the beginning that he was on a crusade and every person in the world with a defective part to their body was grateful to his computer knowledge and dedication, and they didn't even know Will Spencer.

From ninth grade, Libby had been ready to marry Will. But Will had been reluctant to begin a relationship in medical school. He was soon taking engineering courses at the same time, learning how to design computers that made body parts work. Because of his double workload Libby seemed to be less and less important in Will's life.

Even then, Libby was willing to wait. She'd joined in a separate college life with zest, determined to put

Will out of her mind. But it didn't work. She didn't belong there. Will needed her, even if he didn't know it. By the end of her second year she'd been separated from Will long enough, and with Pop's blessing she'd transferred to Atlanta, found an apartment and enrolled in business school.

Two years later she came to the conclusion that the only way she'd ever really spend time with Will was for them to get married. In desperation she approached Will with her plan. When he rejected both her physical advances and her proposal, she'd been devastated.

Then Dixie, her old college roommate, invited her on a ski weekend in Aspen and she'd accepted. That was the weekend she met Stephen Colter, the man who made her see that she was a woman with needs, needs that had to be satisfied by the only man she'd ever love—Will Spencer.

Libby had returned to Atlanta, confused, angry, and uncertain. She knew that she loved Will, but she didn't know how Will felt about her. She didn't call him. She didn't stop by his apartment. It took a week, and a night of drinking, before an unsteady Will Spencer sheepishly turned up at Libby's apartment and announced that he would accept her proposal. It was the following week when they moved in together. June wasn't a good month for the wedding, Will said. He had a symposium. They'd do it later.

Later stretched on for two years, until Libby gave up the idea of the ceremony in the little Methodist Church with the stained-glass windows back in Florida. She settled for a justice of the peace with two strangers as witnesses.

Now, after three years of marriage, Will was standing hesitantly behind her. "Libby, you're sure you'll be all right? I'll stay, if you'd rather."

Libby felt his touch of concern and heard it deepen in his voice. She opened her mouth to hold him back, drew a deep, chastising breath, and changed her pursed lips into a smile.

"No, Will," she said wearily. "Cooking tonight wasn't on my list of pressing issues, anyway. I really do have something else I need to do."

He waited, still not convinced, until the peal of the chime on the living room clock announcing the hour caught his attention. He shifted his weight. Libby knew that he was caught between his impatience to go and his unease over her odd behavior.

"Please go, Will." If she didn't get him out of there, she was going to burst out crying or screaming, she couldn't decide which. "I'm going to take a shower and crawl into bed. I have some serious reading to do." She turned her face and with a forced smile leaned back to receive a gentle, parting kiss.

After he'd left, she turned to survey the aftermath of the great Saran-wrap seduction in the mirror. Dear heavens, the haircut Will had administered made her look like the victim of a moth attack. Molting and no boobs. What a sex symbol! No wonder her seduction plan hadn't worked. For some reason, wisecracks didn't help this time. She couldn't seem to pull her Pollyanna personality out of her hurt.

Libby felt very tired as she slipped on her faded pink quilted housecoat, retrieved Angel Harper's book, and padded barefoot to the kitchen for a cup of hot chocolate. A cup of cocoa had always been her soul-searching food.

As a child, when she'd been in some kind of trouble—usually from trying to imitate Will—Pop would send her to her room. Later, after the house was quiet, and his point had been made, Pop would slip up the stairs with a cup of hot chocolate and they'd talk. Dear Pop. He'd understood back then. How she wished he were here to talk, too. She wasn't at all sure he'd understand the problem she had now. She wasn't sure she understood it herself.

For Libby, it was hard to put the problem into words, but she knew that something was missing. From the first, she'd known that something wasn't quite right, but she hadn't understood what it was. Will seemed happy. What was wrong with her?

Libby placed a record of Christmas carols on the player and as she listened to Elvis' mournful voice sing of a blue Christmas, she carried her cup back to the fire, settled down on the floor with her back against the couch, and opened the book.

"All right, Angel," she warned, "I don't believe all this garbage, but remember I'm in love with a dinosaur. He hasn't been sexually liberated yet and they don't teach loving in medical school. Chapter two had better be more helpful than chapter one."

The staccato sound of water roused Libby to a still dark room. Just as she stretched open her eyelids and forced bleary eyes to read the bedside clock, the alarm went off. Will was already up, taking a shower. She listened for a moment while awareness settled her memory into a hazy recollection of being lifted and carried to bed. She could barely remember gentle hands removing her housecoat and covering her with the spread. Libby stretched once more and snuggled restlessly back into the bed covers, conscious of the feel of soft cotton sheets rubbing against her skin.

Skin? Libby sat straight up. She was stark naked. Not only was she nude, but she, both pillows, and the matching indentions were all on the same side of the bed.

"Damn. Double Damn." She'd slept right through the climatic moment promised in chapter one of Angel Harper's book. She felt edgy, her body tense and out of sorts. It was obvious that she'd slept in Will's arms, that her body had responded to his presence, was still responding. Now he was gone.

The still open bathroom door quivered and Libby quickly leaned back, pulling up the sheet. Will came in, already dressed. He leaned over, and brushed a kiss across her forehead. "Sorry I woke you. I have an early date downtown with the operating room at University Hospital. They're amputating a child's arm, a new procedure I want to watch.

"Afterwards, Pat and I are meeting the board to make a pitch for some more money. We have an idea for a different kind of computerized replacement."

"What time did you get home, Will?" Libby asked, only half hearing what he was saying as she tried to hold him for a moment. "I don't seem to remember coming to bed."

"Not surprised, babe. You were dead asleep hugging a book, with the stereo playing 'White Christmas' over and over, when I came in. The only sound I got out of you was some jabbering about making love with angels.''

Libby watched Will add the matching tweed jacket to the dark wool trousers, tighten his tie, and turn back to her for approval. ''Do I match, Lib? Pat keeps saying that I need to look successful. Wouldn't want the medical world to know they're dealing with a hayseed who has to have his . . . woman buy his clothes.''

''Will, the medical world wouldn't care if you wore a wetsuit and fins, and you know it. It's your mind they're interested in, not the packaging. But,'' she added coyly, ''I like the way you look. I like it very much.''

''Ah shucks, ma'am, you're supposed to,'' he grinned, giving a reasonably good imitation of Gary Cooper. ''I'm your man.'' He started once more out the door, turned and said seriously, ''Still, this is one time I need to look expensive. If I don't look expensive, they won't *think* expensive and this project is going to cost big bucks.''

''Oh? And what project are you about to involve yourself in now? I don't see how you could be more involved than you have been.''

But she was talking to the door. As usual, Will was gone. So much for showing interest in his work. Libby was dressed and fastening her hair on top of her head when she heard footsteps crossing the living room.

''Libby?'' Will stood sheepishly in the doorway, twirling his keys casually in his hand.

''What's wrong?'' Libby asked as she placed the

last pin in her neatly arranged upswept hairdo. She slipped into her low-heeled pumps and turned to pull up the spread on the bed before she realized that Will hadn't answered her.

"Could you lend me your car today, Lib?"

"What's wrong with your truck?"

"I seem to have misplaced it."

"How could anybody misplace a lime-green pickup truck?"

"I think I forgot I had it last night and rode home with Pat. I mean, we were so involved in something that I never even thought about it."

"That figures."

Libby bit back the words of rebuke she was rolling around in her mouth, touched lipstick and blush to her face, and reached for her cape. "All right, Will. You can drop me off and go to your meeting. I'll be in all day anyway, so I won't need it until closing time. But," and she gave him as threatening a look as she could and said with a dare, "you'd better not get involved in what you're doing and forget to pick me up."

"I promise, Libby. I'll pick you up whenever and wherever you say. Just tell me and," he shuffled around anxiously, "hurry, if you can. I'm running late and this is important."

"I'll be ready to leave the bank at five-thirty," Libby reminded him once more as he stopped in front of the bank and she opened the door of her small economy car, "right here under the clock, five-thirty. Please . . ." her voice trailed off. *Please, don't forget me, Will*, she said to herself as she watched him drive away. Waiting for that slow little transit bus that wandered all over creation was something she wasn't interested in doing.

"And don't forget where you park my car," she yelled, knowing that his mind was already down at the medical center. She rapped on the bank window, signaling to the guard inside, who let her in with a smile.

Libby put away her cape and purse and moved to the front of the bank. She looked out the old-fashioned glass window that started waist high and ran almost to the top of the high ceiling, and watched the fluttering of the weather-frayed Christmas bells attached to the street lights. There'd been a drive by the Virginia-Highlands Merchants Association to replace them this fall, but the shopkeepers just hadn't had the kind of year to justify the expense. Business hadn't been good, Libby reflected uneasily, and their bank deposits reflected it.

It was hard to believe that when she'd come to the bank as loan manager three years ago, she'd thought that this community was the most exciting place in the world. As a twenty-four-year-old, small-town girl, fresh out of two disastrous years of college, two sensible years of business school, and two years of working her way up the ladder at another branch of the bank, the array of nationalities of the store owners had seemed very cosmopolitan.

Now, many of the shops were boarded up and just last week the shopkeepers had been horrified by the rumor of the opening of an adult video and bookstore in the middle of the neighborhood where her bank was located.

It was very depressing. Still, as corny as it was,

she felt that this small Atlanta neighborhood was unique. These people were her people and she liked being depended on.

The bank doors opened, and the first of a slow but steady stream of customers hurried in. As assistant manager, Libby settled a dispute in bookkeeping, agreed with the loan officer that a loan extension for the shoe repairmen across the street was probably against the rules but definitely in order, and answered any number of telephone inquiries from people unable to come in.

Every time she looked at the glass windows, or the clear-vinyl covered savings books stacked neatly on her desk, she thought of the plastic wrap last night and cringed. Angel Harper's book might have taken the United States by storm in the seventies, but so far it had been nothing but a big washout for Libby in the nineties.

"Mrs. Spencer, Mrs. Spencer." One of the tellers was calling. "Your phone is ringing."

Libby looked up and shook her head in dismay. She was sitting at the same desk as her phone and she hadn't even heard it ring. She was beginning to act like Will. "Yes?"

"Libby love, Dixie here. I'm headed your way. Meet me at the Old Inn for lunch."

"I'd love to." Libby agreed enthusiastically. "That's close enough to walk. How soon?"

"Twenty minutes?"

In a short time Libby was walking briskly down Highland Avenue, knowing that the wind would probably have her eyes and nose bright red by the time she reached her objective some four blocks away. But the noonday sun had taken the icy bite off the early morning air and Libby was glad she had accepted Dixie's spur-of-the-moment invitation.

The inn's door swung open, moist puffs of air burping out and disappearing as if the building were breathing. Libby slipped inside and scanned the lunchroom crowd, fastening on the hand waving frantically across the room.

"Libby, over here." Dixie Lee Kendall was dark, petite, very southern, and very much the center of attention wherever she was.

Libby blinked in surprise as she moved closer. She almost didn't recognize her friend. "Whatever have you done to your hair?"

The top was cut short in stiff little spikes that looked as if they'd been brushed with gold, while the back hung limply down her neck. To compound the situation, a burnt-gold eyeshadow was skillfully applied to make her dark brown eyes seem permanently surprised. The entire look was amazing.

"Cut it off, love. Do sit down and tell me what you think." Dixie twisted her head back and forth as Libby searched for an appropriate reply.

"Well, all I can honestly say is that it's a good thing you're built like you instead of me, or the waiter would be saying sir, instead of ma'am."

Libby unbuttoned her cape and slid it over the curved slatback chair. She glanced across at the mirrored wall behind them and shook her head at the contrast between the tailored image of her slim skirt and vest and smooth chignon, and the vibrant orange knickers and short, startled haircut on her best friend. Truthfully, Libby didn't know what to say.

"This is what they call the punk look. Exciting, don't you think? Why don't you get yours done? I'll give you the name of the adorable hairdresser who created this, just for me. It will make you feel young again."

"I'll agree that nobody over twenty, outside of the members of a rock band, could wear it. Dixie, you look like somebody plugged you into an electric socket. I can't imagine what Will would say if I came in looking like that."

"I can't imagine what the two of you talk about anyway, Pollyanna and Mr. Clean."

The waiter had appeared silently behind them and served bowls of French onion soup and thick chunks of French bread, which Dixie had already ordered. Libby picked up her spoon in resignation. When you were with Dixie, she ran the show.

"How is the genius doctor?" Dixie asked. "Still bent on computerizing the world's medical problems?"

"Fine." Libby took another sip of the soup, swallowed hard, and tried to think of something witty to say about Will.

"Well, suit yourself about the haircut, but I think it would put a charge in that long tall drink of water you are so enamored of."

The soup threatened to go down the wrong way and Libby coughed noisily behind her napkin. It made her uncomfortable for Dixie to mention Will in that amused tone of voice. She knew what was bothering her was that Dixie was too close to the truth.

"What's it like anyway, being made love to by a

mechanical genius? I mean, does he work out a program for orgasm?''

''Dixie, please! Our sex life is private and he doesn't. I mean he wouldn't.'' She caught herself, realizing as she watched the teasing expression on Dixie's face disappear, that she'd revealed far too much of her distress. Dixie didn't mean anything by her questions. She was just naturally open and outrageous.

''Sorry, Lib. I didn't mean to pry. You know you're my favorite person in the whole world. You and Will are the only good people I know, and the only ones I know who still truly care about each other. Is there trouble in paradise?''

''No, not really. It's just that Will is always so busy and I just seem to get lost in the rush. He's so preoccupied at night, when he comes home at all. We can't even find time to buy a Christmas tree.'' And before she knew it, she'd told Dixie all about her impulsive buy of Angel Harper's book and the disastrous outcome.

''And then he just left, Dixie, and there I was, all sweaty, starving, no food, no lover, and a clip job that makes me look like I'm shedding.'' Libby shook herself, jutted out her chin, and added in a newly determined voice, ''But, you'll be pleased to know that I'm not done yet.''

''I'm not surprised at Will, but you, my little puritan, you shock me. You're coming alive as an old married lady.''

Dixie pushed back her half-empty soup bowl and wiped her mouth, leaving an orange smear on the white napkin. ''Saran Wrap, huh? I read that in a magazine once, but I never actually heard about anybody doing it. I wish I could have seen you.''

Libby heard the laughter in her voice and wished she hadn't blurted out her foolishness. ''Oh, Dixie, don't laugh at me. The book made sense, and it was a best-seller. According to Angel Harper's plan, Will was supposed to take one look and ravish me.''

''And what other little jewels of information did Angel Harper promise to confide?''

''Oh, I don't know. I only started chapter two. I really haven't worked out my full program.''

''You and your programs, Libby. Will is the computer expert, but you're always the one with the program. You think that all you have to do is plan something, follow the plan, and the proper results will automatically come. Has that ever worked with Will?''

''Well, no. But I haven't done too badly so far,'' Libby said, allowing a hint of a pout to creep into her voice in spite of the tight control she was trying desperately to hold on to.

''It won't work like that, my little innocent. Life just sits back and takes potshots at all our carefully thought out little schemes. Nothing is ever neat and fair about love. A woman has to be aggressive, outsmart the man.''

''I know,'' Libby agreed, all pretense at eating abandoned. ''But I am neat and orderly, and I don't interfere. I do make Will happy, I know I do, but I need . . . Oh, I don't know what got into me, or what I need.''

''What you need, my love, is a little fun. Something to really shake up that man of yours. Haven't you ever heard that old expression that the Lord helps those who help themselves?'' She motioned to the waiter and absently signed the check. "I know," Dixie sat straight up with a gleam in her eyes.

"Well, I don't," Libby said too quickly, "and from the look on your face I'm not sure I want to."

"What you need is to . . . to . . . have an affair." Dixie's whole face lit up and Libby shuddered. From past experience, dating all the way back to their first day as college roommates, Libby could always tell when Dixie was plotting something outlandish. She'd get drawn in, and just when they were both faced with impending disaster, Dixie would pull a miracle out of her hat and they'd escape.

"Me? Have an affair? That's impossible. Will would never believe it if I did."

"That's the problem, kid. You've made it too easy for Will. He doesn't need to change anything. He's got everything just like he wants it. You don't make demands, so he doesn't have to respond. Haven't you ever heard that it's the squeaky wheel that gets oiled? We've got to scare him a little."

Dixie had always been considered a bit of a flake, but this might be her most bizarre plan. Libby had to squelch it. "I may be considered totally square, Dixie. Everybody in Atlanta, Georgia, may be swapping lovers, husbands, what have you, but not me. Not only do I not want to have an affair, I wouldn't have the wildest idea how to begin."

"I believe that. I'll bet that you've never even looked at another man since Will Spencer moved next door to you when he was ten and you were six."

"I certainly have. I mean, well there was one."

"I don't believe it. Libby McHanie and another man? No way."

"Well there was; once, anyway."

"Tell me. Tell me, Lib."

"You remember when I went to Snow Valley with you and the rest of the kids from college. I met someone there that I might have liked, very much, but I was too young and inexperienced and I ended up making a fool of myself. I told him I was going back to marry the boy next door. I did."

"You mean I missed something?"

"Well, you were with Butch, or Joe, or somebody. You didn't have time to notice me."

"I do seem to remember that you left pretty suddenly one morning. But I don't think I believe you. Libby McHanie with another man? He must have been pretty exciting. Why'd you run away?"

"That was the problem. He *was* too exciting and before I knew it . . . well, just say I didn't know how to play his game. He made me uneasy. But all that was before Will and I . . . I mean, Will and I weren't even engaged. Don't look at me like that Dixie, the whole weekend was a dumb mistake. I've never loved anyone but Will and you know it. An affair is out of the question," Libby finished lamely.

"What that means is that you let him make love to you once, panicked, and ran. Why, I'll bet he was the first, wasn't he?"

Dixie stopped abruptly and reached out to pat Libby's arm reassuringly. "Don't worry, love, I didn't mean a real affair, though that might do you a world of good. What I had in mind was more pretend.

We'll make Will think you're having one. He may be absent-minded and involved, but he's old-fashioned enough to put his libido in fast forward if he thinks he has competition.''

''I can't do it!'' Libby protested all the way to the door. Definitely not! she told herself all the way back to the bank. Making your husband jealous by pretending to have an affair went out with the dinosaurs, didn't it? An affair, Libby Spencer have an affair? Impossible! Still . . .

"Libby, thank goodness you're back." Lewis Marvin, the bank manager hovered anxiously near the door.

"What's wrong, Lewis? We haven't been robbed, have we? Will!" she cried at the shake of his head. "Something has happened to Will?"

"No," Lewis answered nervously. "I don't know why, Libby, but we've been called downtown to a meeting with Mr. Todd, the chairman of the board. We're due there in less than half an hour so we need to hurry."

"Oh, Lewis, I don't have my car. We'll have to go in yours," she groaned under her breath and followed the elderly man out the backdoor to his automobile. She sensed his unease and began to wonder why they had both been called away from the bank at one time. Something strange was going on.

Lewis fought both the early Friday afternoon exodus and the normal Christmas traffic in jerks and sudden stops. Libby breathed a sigh of relief when he finally pulled into the underground parking area below the building housing Peachtree National Bank headquarters.

Lewis Marvin glanced at his watch. "You don't suppose they've somehow discovered that you're helping all those elderly people by cashing checks and paying their bills when they can't come into the bank, do you?"

"I don't see how they could, Lewis. I only take one of their personal checks, have them fill it out for the amount they need, and take the cash to them at their apartments. It's so much safer for them not to keep large amounts of money. It's my own personal time I use and I can't see how anybody could object. As for paying the bills and balancing their checkbooks, they're old and either don't know how, or can't see well enough to do it any longer."

"Libby, you don't have to convince me. I know how much they depend on you, and they are our oldest customers, but I can't think of any other reason for us to be called in."

"Good afternoon, Mr. Marvin, Mrs. Spencer. I'm Mrs. Hadley, Mr. Todd's assistant. You're the last two."

The last two what? Libby wanted to ask as she followed Mr. Marvin into the conference room. She only wished she'd had time to comb her hair and freshen her makeup. This was her first time to be summoned downtown and the windy walk at lunch made her less confident than she might have wished.

Mr. Todd nodded and stood. "Gentlemen, and Ms. Spencer. As chairman of the board, I've called you here to announce a move that will directly affect your futures, as well as that of the bank. Effective January first, a little more than two weeks from now, Peachtree National Bank and its three branches will merge with First Windsor Trust.''

There was a ripple of sound as the listeners took in the information.

''For the moment,'' Mr. Todd went on, ''everything will continue as usual. However, I am told that there will be a number of upcoming policy changes in the general operation of the bank and its personnel. There will be someone coming in from corporate headquarters to coordinate the changeover.''

There was another pause. Mr. Todd took a nervous breath and dropped his stiff composure for a moment. ''I know this comes as a shock to all of you. I can say that I wish it had not become necessary.'' The waver in his voice turned hard and he finished in a crisp voice that brought a chill to the room. ''For the moment, we will simply continue to operate under the policies that have served us well since my grandfather founded Peachtree National Bank. Thank you for coming.''

''I hate it!'' Libby fumed on the way out. ''First Windsor Trust gobbles us up like Pac Man swallowing dots on the game board. The neighborhood bank is disappearing. The neighborhood shops are disappearing. Even the neighborhoods are disappearing. Everything is changing and I don't want it to.''

Lewis Marvin smiled and patted Libby absently on the shoulder. ''That's part of life, Libby. Facing problems makes us grow, or so they say. But, between you and me, I'm glad I don't have to worry about it much longer.'' He was only months away from retirement.

"But what will happen to our bank, to me?''

"Don't worry, Libby, you and I both know you've been running the bank for the last year. You're the assistant manager and you're more than qualified to take my place. You know our customers as nobody else possibly could. I'll put that in my recommendation, if anyone asks my opinion. I'm sure you'll be fine.''

"I hate what's happening and I will worry.'' And she did. Peachtree National was family; it was a benevolent parent caring for its young. What would their customers do if the bank changed its way of doing business, or what was more frightening, closed entirely?

It wasn't her own future she was concerned about. With her experience, she felt certain she could find another job in the banking community, very probably making a great deal more money than she was making now. It was all the people, the elderly, the small business owners that she worried about.

At five-thirty, Libby closed and locked her desk and watched the last employee leave before pulling on her bright red cape. She looked around, checking the empty bank once more. She loved the rich old smell of the empty building, the polished floors that echoed when she walked across them, and the gleaming brass rails that had to be buffed each morning. Nothing new or modern, but it had character and she felt a sadness that it might be coming to an end.

First Windsor Trust would have to be told about

the clients who had come here as children and now brought their grandchildren in. Old, out-of-date, and simple, Peachtree National had a heart. Libby didn't want to think that it might be the end of an era.

She waved to the janitorial crew moving in behind her and slipped out the front door, glancing up at the clock as she did every night.

The clock. Will. Libby remembered with a start that Will was picking her up and he was already late. She should have waited inside where it was warm. The clock changed from the time to the temperature and Libby shivered. The temperature dropped a degree while she was standing there. Letting her back inside would be against normal procedure and even the cleaning crews had been cautioned against falling into tricks to open up. Any other time Libby would have remembered that she was being picked up and she would have waited inside. But today had shattered her routine.

The lunch date with Dixie and all that nonsense about having an affair had started it. Then the news about the bank merger had made her forget everything else. She paced back and forth, mind still whirling with questions, feet numbing now with cold as the minutes passed. Pent-up emotion finally spilled over and Libby got mad.

"Suppose I just don't go home, Will Spencer?" she said as a startled shopper stopped in passing. Libby shook her head at his questioning glance and marched off toward the bus stop. "You probably wouldn't even miss me. The bank probably won't miss me either."

Traffic in the street beside her was bumper-to-bumper, brakes screaming, horns blaring rudely. Peace on earth, she thought with bitter disappointment. Her life was changing. She remembered the Christmases she'd spent with Will, always busy, almost an unwelcome interruption in his schedule. She sighed, knowing that she was dumping all her disappointment on Will, knowing that he never meant to make her unhappy. He would be honestly surprised if he knew how depressed she was.

Snow Valley came unbidden into her thoughts. Snow Valley and Stephen and the first time that Will made love to her. Being with Will had been wonderful, all the excitement and anticipation, making slow, sweet love, just being together. Loving Will had been what she wanted then and forever. She'd never been more sure. Where had it all gone?

If Will was even aware that it was Christmas, she didn't know it. Tomorrow was Saturday. Perhaps he would have some time to help select a tree. They'd stop at the inn for breakfast and spend the whole day together—if Will had time. Of course, if he couldn't find time to pick her up or call to say he was going to be late, there was no reason to assume he'd be able to work on a Christmas tree.

Libby knew that she was wallowing in self-pity. But, she thought, with a pout, she was entitled. It wasn't that she was unhappy. It wasn't hormones. It wasn't intentional on Will's part. It was Christmas. And Libby was emotional about Christmas. She always had been. Christmas meant family and love. Christmas meant Will. Except Will didn't seem to notice her anymore.

Just ahead on her left was Christmas House, an

old-fashioned Victorian mansion playing peek-a-boo with the stark box buildings and offices around it. A string of stars bordered a blinking sign in the window. Behind the sign she could see the brightly decorated Christmas trees. She turned impulsively and went in. At least this kind of impulse wouldn't get her in the kind of trouble that Angel Harper's book had.

Only a few shoppers, or browsers, or spirit-seekers were in the twinkling shop. Sugerplum trees, trees strung with starlight and angel hair, tall trees, pink trees, trees of every child's dream made the house a wonderland. Libby wandered around, strangely dissatisfied.

Finally, in the back corner, around an archway, almost hidden among all the newer displays, she came upon an old-fashioned English Christmas village, enclosed in nose-smudged glass. Light spilled out of the quaint village shops into the snow-frosted street peopled with tiny carolers and shoppers. If I could only be there, my arm tucked under the elbow of that tall, bearded gentleman lifting his hat in greeting, she thought. So mesmerized was she that it was some time before she noticed the reflection of the tall, bearded man beside her.

Then he spoke. "Libby?"

She turned. "Stephen? She couldn't believe it. "I'm surprised. You recognized me?" she asked in a voice far too breathless.

"I would always know you."

He was still tall and confident, and being close to him took her voice away, just as it had six years ago.

"You've grown a beard," was all she could say. She wished she was Dixie. Dixie would know what to say to the man from her past, the only man she'd ever . . . Damn it, why had Will forgotten her tonight? It was almost like an omen.

"Come," Stephen took her arm. "Let's go next door and have a cup of coffee and talk."

She was speechless as he led her to the corner of what turned out to be a dark and intimate bar, and she was afraid. She'd turned away from him once because she hadn't known how to be with such a man. Vibrant, alive, exciting, he'd been going somewhere she wasn't sure she wanted to go.

"How about your life? Did you go back home and marry the boy next door like you said?"

"Yes," she whispered.

"And did it give you what you wanted?"

"Well, almost."

"You know I went to your college friends and asked for you. But they didn't, or wouldn't, tell me where you were, and I didn't know where to look."

"You did?" She hadn't known and, truthfully, she was glad she hadn't. And so it went, the superficial chatter. "Are you still looking for your first million dollars?"

"Nope. But I'm getting there. Any children?"

"No."

The feeling between Stephen and her was still as strong as it had been that weekend when they'd first met. She'd been miserable, choked with self-pity. *Why hadn't Will wanted her in Atlanta with him? Why wasn't Will here with her? Why did he never seem to have time for fun?*

At the resort, she'd been sitting in the windowseat looking out at the snow-covered valley, regretting her rash decision, when Stephen sought her out.

"It's easy to be lonely, even in a crowd, isn't it?"

Looking up at the man wearing the dark blue turtleneck sweater and jeans that hugged his body like a second skin, she thought he was the most striking, intriguing man she'd ever seen.

"Sometimes," she agreed and turned to look back at the skiers, afraid to let him know how shaken she was by the unexpected physical reaction of her body.

He stood there for a time, looking past her, breathing that even, relaxed breath that made her all the more aware of his nearness. "I'm alone, too. Do you suppose we might share our time, purely as a method of self-defense, of course."

"Self-defense?" In spite of her reluctance, she turned, drawn to this self-assured man who could have stepped right out of a *Playgirl* magazine centerfold.

"Of course. If you're not paired off within an hour of arrival, you're either fair game for every sex-starved wallflower in the lodge, or you're forced to find your own wallspace and join them as an on-looker. This way, we're both accepted as part of the 'in' group, whether or not we carry it any further."

And she had agreed, hardly knowing what that meant. By the time they had spent half the evening together, talking, dancing, simply looking at each other, as they absorbed the intimate aura of physical awareness that circled the two of them, it seemed perfectly natural to nod her agreement when he walked her to her cabin.

When he'd kissed her, she'd responded and quickly moved into the sensual throes of passion she'd only read about and wished for. He'd taken her to bed and she'd gone freely and expectantly. The coming together for the first time hadn't been like she'd read in books, but Stephen had been romantically tender and caring and she'd liked it, liked it very much. When he was ready to leave for the slopes the next morning, he'd hesitated, come back and kissed her gently.

"Thank you, Libby. I never expected to be the first, but I'm so touched. It will be better next time. I promise to make it very good for you so that someday when you find the man you want to marry you'll be ready."

She'd stayed there for a long time after he'd gone, refusing to hear what he'd said. What a fool she'd been, thinking that his need for her had meant he was in love with her. She'd been the dinosaur then. She'd given herself to him and he was preparing her for his leaving. Quickly, she'd dressed and composed a note telling him she was going back home and would marry the boy next door. He would remember her only as that pleasant weekend at Snow Valley.

She hadn't been able to find Dixie. But she'd given her friends the excuse that she wasn't well and left, totally crushed, and more alone than she'd ever been. For the next long week she'd hidden behind closed doors, and ignored the phone, until she realized that Stephen probably wasn't looking for her at all. Then Will had come.

"Why did you run away that weekend?" Stephen's question called her back to the uncertainty of the present, where muted voices, the sound of Christmas carols, and the clink of ice swirled around her.

"I was afraid, afraid of what you made me feel, and I didn't know how to handle a casual affair. There was someone I'd always expected to marry. You were a surprise."

"It wasn't so casual, you know," he said in a strangely reticent voice. "You were very special and you scared the hell out of me, too. I'd never been with anybody like you and your trust wiped me out. To put it simply, I blew it."

"I was?" She took a sip of the coffee he'd ordered for her and tried to still the tremor in her voice. She ought to stop this. She belonged to Will now. They were married. Stephen belonged to the past.

"Please don't, Stephen. I'm married to the man I've been in love with since I was six years old. When I met you, something had happened. Our relationship wasn't going anywhere. He was in medical school and didn't have time for me. I thought he didn't love me, and then I met you the very next weekend. I guess I was vulnerable and you came along at the right time. That's all there was to it."

"No," he contradicted. "It was more than that, at least for me. Somehow, you reached out to me. Later, when I came back to tell you, you were gone and I didn't know what to do. I didn't even know your last name. My company transferred me to North Carolina and I didn't have enough time to keep up the search." His eyes turned from the bright crinkly blue she remembered to a deep cloudy color, and she felt magnetically drawn into them. Everything seemed to fade away, leaving only the present and Stephen

Colter, and the unyielding power he seemed to have over her.

Their hands accidentally touched and the shock took her breath away. She couldn't look at him. Suddenly, the memory of Dixie's wild scheme to convince Will that she was having an affair cut through her like a shaft of ice and she began to tremble. Something about Stephen and the confusion of the day had come together in a physical reaction that was making it hard to breathe.

She seemed frozen in time, halfway between that weekend at Snow Valley and the present. It was wrong she knew, but she was responding to Stephen all over again and she couldn't stop herself from wanting to know that he was feeling the same thing. But she couldn't ask. Instead, she held her breath in confusion.

Stephen barely touched her hand with his fingertips and the touch burned like fire. She backed away, bolting to her feet in the sudden panic of awareness.

"I have to go."

"Have dinner with me, Libby? I haven't even found out where you work, or how to reach you. I don't want to lose you a second time."

"No. I can't," she blurted out, tilting the tiny table in her haste to escape. "I mean, I'd rather not. I'll miss my bus." She walked rapidly out of the intimate darkness, seeking, needing the feel of cold on cheeks she knew were hot and flushed.

"Why are you so upset, Libby? I didn't mean to frighten you. Forget what happened. It's Christmas and I'm in town alone and you're an old friend.

That's all.'' He followed her out the door and into the now vacant street.

As they walked slowly toward the bus stop, she began to feel foolish. She'd built the whole incident into some kind of magic spell, imagining things that weren't there. He was just an old friend she happened to run into again. They had simply talked, though she couldn't remember what they'd said. She'd go home and tell Will and they'd laugh about it.

Just as she reached the corner, her bus pulled up and opened its doors. Gratefully, she stepped aboard and turned back with a timid wave to the man standing below as it began to move.

She worked her way to the back of the bus and found a seat. Her head had begun to ache. She forced her eyes straight ahead and told herself that he'd invited her to dinner and she'd refused. There was no way he could call her. That was the end of that.

But the guilty feeling persisted all the way home and she felt her secret meeting was written across her in neon letters. It was all Will's fault. If *he'd* picked her up as he should have, this never would have happened. But nothing happened, she argued, nothing at all. Then why did she want to hurry back to the street corner and . . .

Libby flung open the door to a dark, empty apartment. Will wasn't home. She couldn't even tell him what happened. She didn't know whether to laugh or cry. Unbuttoning her cape, Libby pitched it across the bed to the floor on the other side, leaving it in a wrinkled heap as she headed for the bathroom. She turned on the shower and swallowed two headache tablets from the medicine cabinet while the room filled with steam. Her clothes soon joined her cape and she stepped wearily under the peppery jabs of hot water.

"Lib! Lib! Where are you? Guess what. You'll never believe what happened to me today." Will ripped through the bedroom, uncharacteristically yelling all the way.

Libby felt the shower door flung open behind her, turned and leveled an icy glare. "Do you mean before or after you left me standing on the corner in the six-o'clock rush with the temperature dropping by the minute?"

"Ah, Lib. I'm sorry, but when you hear, you'll forget all about it."

"I doubt it." This was a new Libby, giving voice to pent-up emotion in a way she never had before.

The glow of boyish excitement faded slowly from Will's face and he blinked rapidly, dropped his arms in a gesture of defeat. When he spoke, Libby caught a glimpse of something more than disappointment.

"You're right, Libby. If I hadn't forgotten my truck, I wouldn't have borrowed your car and you wouldn't have had to ride the bus. It was unforgivable of me." He turned away dejectedly.

Libby turned off the water, dried herself quickly, glanced ruefully in the mirror at the splotchy haircut, and slipped into her old quilted robe. She was beginning to regret railing at Will. She was taking out her confusion on him. But the happenings of the day were still whirling around like a hazy nightmare that refused to be laid aside. She wrapped a towel turban-style around her wet hair and went after him. This time she'd make him understand.

"Will, I'm sorry. I . . ." Libby came to an abrupt stop. Will wasn't alone. On the kitchen stool sat the most forlorn, solemn little boy she'd ever seen.

"Here she is, Tiger, your temporary mama. Isn't she a doll? She's very glad you're going to stay with us for awhile. Of course, she won't be able to talk to you because she doesn't speak Vietnamese and you don't speak English."

Will was rummaging through the refrigerator, piling food on the counter before the wide-eyed child. "Right now, she's mad at Will because he left her stranded downtown and she had to ride a bus home. But when she gets to know you, she'll get over it." Will talked to the child, pausing now and then to emphasize a word and glance up at Libby.

Libby was absolutely speechless. The child didn't move. He seemed frozen before Libby's shocked reaction. She examined him with a detachment she wouldn't have thought possible. About six years old, she'd judge, malnutrition and heaven knows what else had dampened both his size and his spirit. He clasped a paper bag tightly with one hand. And then she noticed . . .

"Will, he has no arm. What happened?" Libby realized she was still standing with her arms over her head, tucking the towel into a turban. When she dropped them, the child grinned timidly and said quite distinctly,

"Mama?"

"Mama?" Libby echoed and began to laugh. It was too much. First, Angel Harper led her into making a fool of herself. Then, when she might have enjoyed the seduction she planned, she'd slept straight through it. Next, Dixie suggested an affair, which very nearly became a reality when she met her only old flame, on the same day she found that her job was in jeopardy. The laughter became more intense and she tried to catch her breath to explain to a thoroughly shocked Will that she wasn't losing her mind, she was simply spaced out and giddy with pent-up emotion.

"It's okay, Libby," Will said gently, holding out his hands helplessly. "I mean, I know this comes as a shock to you. That's what I was trying to tell you, I mean about Tiger here."

"Shock?" Libby managed to gasp as she dropped to her knees, holding her aching sides. "Nothing that happens the rest of my life will be a shock to me after today."

Libby wanted to stop. She wanted to put her arms around the frightened little boy. She wanted to say that she wasn't hysterical over him. But she couldn't seem to stop her bizarre behavior.

Will looked puzzled. The boy simply watched in frozen amazement. The doorbell rang. Libby sat where she was, trying to breathe deeply as she waited to see what else was ready to, as Dixie had put it, take potshots at her nice, safe, peaceful little world.

Will went to the door, opened it, and said something, before coming back to the kitchen carrying a long white box tied with a red bow.

"They're for you, babe. Something from a secret admirer?" He gave her a long look, laid the box on the floor beside her, and went back to his sandwich making.

Libby stared at the box, a feeling of disaster hovering over her as she untied the ribbon. Inside the box were a dozen perfect, delicate pink roses and a card. She picked it up, closed her eyes, and prayed. Please let it be from Santa Claus.

The strong black handwriting on the card read, *For yesterday, tomorrow, and you.*

THREE

"Where's the mustard, babe? Tiger likes mustard on his bologna sandwiches."

"Uh, in the cabinet." Libby's fingertips felt seared as she closed them frantically around the florist's card, slid it casually down her hip, and slipped it into her housecoat pocket.

"Where?"

How had he found her? She must have left something in the bar, or he must have followed her. It didn't make sense. She picked up the flower box, steadied her legs beneath her, and leaned weakly against the wall.

"Who?"

"Who, what?" Libby felt like a wind-up toy soldier as she moved woodenly to the pantry for a container, finally settling for an empty gallon jug.

"Who sent the flowers?"

"I don't know. There was no signature. I thought you might have done it."

" 'Fraid not. Guess I ought to have, after what I did, forgetting you and all.'' He looked sheepishly at Libby, his forgetfulness giving her a temporary respite from any inquisition he might have put forth. "Put them somewhere and come help me feed Tiger here."

At the mention of the child, her eyes went to him, and she began to regret her outburst. Poor child. He didn't understand. It wasn't fair to subject him to her sudden burst of hysteria. As she searched for a way to reach him, the boy began to move about, a worried expression lining his small round face.

"What's your problem, Tiger?" Will went on in an unusually jovial manner. "Hunger getting to you? I'm almost done here."

The boy moved in jerks, drawing his scrawny legs together tightly.

"Will, I think your Tiger needs a sandbox, rather quickly."

Will stopped for a moment before he understood her meaning, caught the child under his arm and headed for the bathroom.

Libby drew in a deep breath, held it for a moment, then let slowly out, searching her mind for a reasonable explanation for the flowers, the flowers that Will would surely question, sooner or later. She quickly filled the jar with water, crammed the long stems in the container, and placed it on the entrance hall table by the door, where it was out of sight.

Will was carrying on a jovial one-sided conversation in the bathroom. His absence gave her a few precious minutes to get over her shock. She forced herself to concentrate on something solid, concrete, something she could touch and feel. Will's sandwich makings spilled over the counter like the aftermath of a little league picnic and she turned gratefully to it.

By the time Will and the child entered the kitchen once more, she had set the table, poured tall glasses of milk, and placed the curious looking sandwiches on small paper plates.

"Boy, look at the feast, Tiger." Will swung the child into the air, placed him in a chair, and moved him up to the table. "Nope, won't do, too low." He looked around for a moment, grabbed the telephone book and slid it under him. "Now eat."

The child watched warily as Will sat down, picked up his sandwich and took an oversize bite, chewing lustily. "Eat," Will directed, taking another bite.

Libby watched in amazement at the extraordinary behavior of the man she'd lived with for five years. He was eating his sandwich like a comic character in a silent movie.

"Close your mouth, Libby, and sit down," he said out of the corner of his mouth. "You need to act natural."

"Natural?" she repeated lightly, with a forced smile. "I should act natural when I'm watching you act like an idiot in front of a strange child who . . ."

"Libby! Have some milk." He took a big gulp and lifted his glass at the child.

". . . is scared to death and hanging on to a paper bag, like it's full of gold and we're trying to steal it."

Will's shocked expression was no greater than Libby's own astonishment at herself. "Libby, I thought

I could count on you to understand. You spend all your time helping all those old people. It seemed only natural to think you might have a little compassion for a six-year-old child who lost his arm in some god-awful way that still gives him nightmares. I guess I was wrong. Just go and do whatever it was I interrupted.''

His words were pleasant and delivered through lips that smiled, but Libby knew that he was angry, very angry, and she was astonished. She wanted to protest but she couldn't. He was right. She was behaving abominably. She was jealous and spiteful toward a child who deserved more.

Finally, she turned stiffly and padded barefoot to the bedroom where she began to dry her hair. Her actions became a planned move to distance herself from the child and Will while she got herself together. The disappointment in Will's voice lingered in her mind and a curious dread crept over her. She couldn't seem to think. Anyone would feel compassion for a child. Any other time she would be reaching out, offering comfort, trying to take away his fear.

But this time she couldn't control herself. All she could see was that Will had time for a child, when he didn't have time for her. Half of her knew that she was behaving abominably. The other half refused to relent.

It wasn't fair. At every turn she was shoved aside. Will had simply dismissed her while he stayed in the kitchen carrying on a non-stop conversation with a six-year-old child who couldn't speak English. Everything and everybody was more important than she was. She put on her oldest flannel nightgown, jerked back the covers, and flopped down on the bed.

Libby turned out the light, punched up her pillow, and curled up in a tight little ball under the quilted comforter. She knew she was acting like a spoiled child, but she simply couldn't go back to the kitchen and listen to Will keep up his one-sided conversation. That child had probably heard more from Will in one night than she heard in a month. And he still didn't know about the bank merger. Her problems weren't important anyway.

But was it Will she was worried about? Or was it the flowers and her guilt that were making her crazy? As long as she focused her anger on Will, she didn't think about the flowers, or her emotionally shattering meeting with the sender, Stephen Colter. Just the thought of his name took her breath away and she began to tremble.

What on earth was she going to do?

Libby came suddenly awake. She shook the sleep from her eyes as her ears took in the terrifying cry that pierced her entire being. She could hear the sound of Will's heavy breathing beside her. The shrieking gave way to sad, heartrending sobs that faded into a low, painful moan.

The child. Libby didn't stop to analyze her actions. She simply flew across the darkened room, down the hall to the tiny second bedroom where the sound originated. She flicked on the soft light in the entrance and moved across the room to the bed where she could see a small circular knot in the covers. The moan changed once more into a loud, deep hiccup.

"What's wrong, little one?" she whispered softly, reaching out to touch the pitiful figure.

At the sound of her voice the sobbing increased once more and Libby began to become alarmed. She didn't know where or how, but she knew the child was in some horrible place, or state of being that she could only try to imagine. Libby started to get Will, but something drew her back to the child. She knew that he couldn't keep this up. In the hospital, Will came instantly awake. At home he could sleep through a hurricane.

Finally, in desperation, Libby reached down, pulled back the cover and lifted the iron-stiff little boy, who still clutched the wrinkled paper bag, in her arms. She looked around for a moment, then dropped down into the rocking chair in the corner, pulling him close to her. The rocking chair had been a wedding present from her grandmother, meant to be used to rock her own child, the child she and Will were to have some day, not this strange child that Will had temporarily adopted.

Libby could feel his heart pounding as he burrowed into the crevice under her neck. She rocked, stroking his thin little arm as she clicked back and forth. After a time she began to hum. Suddenly, she was back in her own bed, awaking in the darkness from the terror of some nameless nightmare to the gentle stroke of Pop's big hands. He'd sing, often making up the song as the occasion demanded. Now, Pop was gone and Libby was the singer and she, too, began to improvise as she sang, improvise words for a small boy who couldn't know what she was saying.

When at last he fell into a peaceful sleep, his grasp loosened on the bag and it dropped to the floor. Libby opened it carefully and held it to the light so that she could see. He'd stuffed a crumb of his sandwich inside, along with a whistle, a deck of playing cards, an odd-shaped piece of wood, and some string. His treasures, she thought. The bag contained all the things important to him. She closed it quietly, lifted him gently back into bed, and lay down beside him, telling herself that it was simply a precaution against any further disturbance, though she knew it was her own nightmares she was pushing away.

She might tell herself that she resented the attention Will gave the child, but she could never resent a child. She knew too well how it had felt to want to be loved.

By seven, Libby waked. The child seemed relaxed in sleep now, and she felt a tightening of her heartstrings at the sight of the empty space where an arm ought to have been. She slipped stealthily back to her own bed with Will. She didn't know what Will expected of her, but an attachment to a child who would never be hers was a problem that she couldn't deal with now.

Resolutely, she pushed the boy out of her mind. It was Will's problem to solve, she told herself as she pulled up the blanket. The child has family somewhere. All we're doing is helping while Will works with the hospital on a replacement for his arm. This wouldn't be the first child Will had worked with. But it was the first one he'd brought home for a weekend.

When she opened her eyes again, the apartment was deadly quiet and bright winter sunlight threw fan-like stripes across the bed. She struggled upright, stretching her shoulders tensely, wondering where Will and the child were. She stumbled sleepily to her feet, forced open her eyes as she pulled on the quilted robe, and splashed water on her face. After she'd brushed her teeth, she found only an empty kitchen, the remains of corn flakes, banana peels, and spilled milk on the kitchen table along with a note that said she was to be ready for big doings when the two men in her life returned.

"Two men." A shudder ran down her backbone, and she glanced around, wondering what had happened to the flower box she'd left standing in the corner. Surely, Will hadn't taken it away, or had he? She wondered briefly if he could go to the florist and demand to know the sender, the identity of the other man in his wife's life. You're a fool, Libby, she thought sternly. Will isn't interested in anything except that child. Don't fret your guilty conscience and your hidden desires into a complex of some kind. She forced herself to concentrate on the present and began to tidy the mess Will had left behind.

Libby was standing at the window, blowing into her cup of hot coffee, when she saw Will, arms full of packages, and the child, still carrying his paper bag, pile out of Will's green truck and start down the walk. The bright December sunlight was deceptive, she decided, as she saw a sudden swirl of wind ruffle Will's pale blonde hair.

Through the patches of fog her breath had painted on the windowpane, she saw that both Will and the boy sported new, bright blue down jackets. The only difference was the one scarlet mitten Tiger was wearing. She felt a pang as she saw the empty sleeve swing in the breeze. Apparently, Will had remembered where he'd left the truck. From the packages, she knew they had been shopping and she was sorry for a moment that they'd left her behind.

Will's lanky frame moved in long gliding steps, intentionally slowing, as spindly short legs flew alongside. She watched their progress, suddenly seeing another set of skinny legs stretching to keep up with a younger Will—her own. He'd always been kind, in spite of the teasing of the other boys, at her tagging along. When the girls had played dolls and house, Libby had caught frogs and watched for shooting stars through toy telescopes with Will. When Will broke his leg riding his bicycle, Libby had broken her arm the very next day on her skateboard. Pop had laughed and said, if Will Spencer had jumped in the fire, she'd have been right behind.

They'd shared their first kiss and Will had been very serious when he decided that examining a real live body was much better for a doctor than paperwork. Later, when he was in medical school, she'd told herself that Will's holding back hadn't been from reluctance, or from the strict discipline that got him through in record time—that it had been a sweet promise of what was to come when he was out from under the pressure of his work. She just never expected to find herself waiting still. But that was a long time ago. And this—this was now.

New excitement washed across her and suddenly she wanted to be ready, ready for whatever plans Will had made for the day. Flying to the bedroom she pulled on faded jeans, a thick knitted red sweater, and boots. She was braiding her hair when she heard their return.

"Are you up, babe?" Will called out over the rustling of paper bags being emptied. "Come and see what Tiger and I bought." Will's excitement spilled over and she smiled in return. Only a tiny spiteful part of herself wanted that excitement to be for her. She took a look at the boy's face and chastised herself for such pettiness.

"Looks like you got an early start."

"Up with the chickens," Will grinned. "I know," he paused, and looked across the bed at her with a look of pride on his face, "that you didn't get much rest last night, so Tiger and I let you sleep in."

"Surely this child has a name," Libby said, taking a genuine interest in the solemn-faced little boy. "Libby, Libby." She knelt in front of him and pointed to herself. "Libby." Then she touched Will with her extended finger. "Will."

"Will." The tiny hesitant voice copied, then glanced slowly up at the man whose name he again sounded out. "Will?"

"Yes, Will." Libby nodded, pointed to the child's chest and raised her eyebrows. Silence. Once more she went around. "Libby . . . Will, and . . ."

"Tigrrr," he supplied with a grin.

"All right," Will laughed. "Tiger it is. Grab your coat and hat, Lib. Tiger and I will make a pit stop and then we're going out to lunch and to pick out a Christmas tree."

"A Christmas tree?" It seemed a lifetime ago that she'd wondered if Will would find time to work a tree into his schedule. Now it seemed he'd thrown the schedule away. She felt laughter well up inside. Maybe this child was what they'd needed. Maybe he could reach Will in a way she couldn't. Whatever the reason, she intended to enjoy the day. It was Christmas, the season to forgive.

The Christmas traffic merged with the normal traffic jam of cars entering and leaving the Varsity. The world's largest drive-in restaurant was always busy on Saturday, but this day was worse than usual. Tiger sat close to Will, looking out the window in frozen awe. Will parked the truck and they braved the chill wind to dash inside.

As they stood in line at the order counter, Tiger crouched between them, impatient to see the source of the short-order jargon being yelled back and forth by the complex of nationalities behind the counter. Will took the tray filled with chili dogs, fried peach pies, and the famous Varsity orange drinks, and led the way to a table. In the crush of people, they were quickly separated and the child let out a cry of fear, clinging to Libby's legs.

"Tiger, Tiger," she said as she swung him up over her hip, oblivious to the curious looks of passersby, and soothed his fear as she threaded her way through the crowd to the table and Will.

"Will," he cried happily and allowed Libby to slide him into the empty space between them. Tiger followed Will's lead and quickly demolished a chili dog and a pie before leaning back to practice every new word he learned, to the amusement of the people at the surrounding tables. Libby caught his secret motion in slipping his Varsity paper plate into the ever-present paper bag.

The time passed quickly and pleasantly for the three. As they started back to the truck, Libby's eyes met Will's and an unexpected spark of electricity flew between them. Later, as they drove down Peachtree Street, examining the Christmas tree lots, she felt the touch of Will's arm across the back of the seat as he unconsciously ran his fingers across her shoulder.

"What'ya think, babe, Honest Nick's trees? Why not? Who'd be more trustworthy at Christmas than a dealer named Honest Nick? Shall we take a closer look?"

Tiger clutched Will's hand and followed him down the tree-lined paths, still bewildered but trusting. Libby hardly saw the trees, so conscious was she of the simmering excitement of Will's touch. His arm was casually draped across her shoulder and when he turned to say something she could feel the warmth of his breath.

Finally, he stood before a very tall fir tree in the back corner of the lot. "This is it, the perfect tree. Just what we're looking for." With one arm Will swung Tiger up, planting him on his hip, pulling Libby close with the other. He touched his lips to hers as though he was planting a promise of what was to come. For a moment his tongue parted her lips and she felt a tremor wrack her body and she leaned into the intimacy his kiss now demanded.

"Will," the high-pitched little voice cried out. "Will."

Almost reluctantly, Will pulled back and gave his attention once more to the boy. *Forget about him*, Libby wanted to say. *I need you, too*. Then guiltily, she dropped her eyes and tapped Tiger on the chest and said, "Look, Tiger, this is a Christmas tree. Say tree . . . tree." She didn't know what was wrong with her, being jealous of a child. It was just that ever since she'd seen Stephen, it was as if she needed Will's love in a way that she couldn't explain.

When Tiger was satisfied that he was no longer left out of the moment, he smiled and surprised Libby by repeating both new words. "Christmas tree."

They paid far too much for the tree, put it in the back of the pickup truck, and started home. Libby was convinced that it wouldn't fit in the living room. But she didn't care. They'd decorate it on the roof if it would keep Will's attention focused on home.

"By the way," Will asked casually, "did you lose any?"

"Lose any what?"

"Weight? That's what you said you were doing, wrapped up in that plastic."

"Uh, yes. I mean enough," she answered, hoping he didn't plan to carry that train of thought any further.

"Good, because I plan to check you out thoroughly, later on. If there is a spot that needs adding to or taking away, I'll be the one to decide."

Libby felt her heart leap and a blush creep across her face. Will never made remarks like that, and while she knew Tiger didn't understand, she was curiously embarrassed and excited by it. Her mind wondered, but her body seemed to race forward, trembling in anticipation.

Will made a quick stop at the corner deli and came out with packages that he carefully placed under his feet, giving a warning not to even guess what he had planned for the rest of the day.

"You bring Tiger and unpack the decorations," Will instructed, "while I see about this fir masterpiece."

Libby glowed in the remembered aftermath of Will's unexpectedly passionate kiss in the Christmas tree lot. Tiger joined in, helping her move the boxes of decorations. By the time Will had pulled the tree up the steps, the room was already bright with red, green, and silver.

"I'm afraid you're right, Libby," Will agreed. "We've either got to raise the roof or shorten the tree." When Libby finally located Will's misplaced saw, they took two feet off the bottom and clamped the tree into the stand. Will let Tiger pour water into the base and together they covered it with the bright red Christmas skirt Libby had made the first year they'd spent together.

Libby watched Will as he tangled the tree lights hopelessly, her lips lifted in a smile that fastened on him with increased frequency as they worked.

"Will, what do you know about the child? How did you manage to bring him home?" Libby took the lights and strung them across the floor, plugging them in to check for burn-outs before they were draped around the tree.

"Not a whole lot, I'm afraid," he confessed ruefully. "He was sent to the children's hospital by a troop of marines, I think, or maybe it was army. Anyway they ran across him in a hospital just after his arm was amputated and decided to help him out.

Nobody seems to know just what happened and he doesn't speak enough English to tell us, even if he was inclined to. The note that came with him suggests that he has closed it out of his mind and may never remember.''

"But what about his family?" The tree was beginning to sparkle with a shimmering of tiny lights now. Tiger sat, watching in wonder as Will wound strands around to the top.

"The state department official handling the case told the hospital admissions office that there are several older children and a mother.''

"Beautiful," Libby said as they stood back to survey the effect of the lights. She stood beside Will, enjoying the warm feeling of togetherness that she'd longed for. Looking back, Libby decided that somewhere during the last years while Will had been so immersed in his research and she'd been climbing the ladder of success at the bank, they'd put themselves on the back burner and never really gotten back on track again. If she could just hold on to this, maybe . . .

"What next, babe? Let's give Tiger here a job.''

Ornaments were uncovered and while Libby directed, Will and Tiger hung them. If the bottom was a little top-heavy, nobody would notice, she thought. Although he couldn't understand what they were doing, Tiger threw himself into the spirit and the tree came alive with sparkling lights, colored balls, and little creatures Libby had collected through the years.

"What about the rest of my question," Libby

asked. "I mean, how did you manage to end up with a houseguest?"

"I couldn't see leaving him in that hospital for the weekend when his surgery isn't even scheduled until the week after Christmas. You don't mind, do you, Lib?" He twisted his head around, lifted his eyebrows, and shrugged with that endearing little-boy innocence that always got to her and she laughed when she realized she was already shaking her head no. And she didn't mind, she realized. The child seemed to be a catalyst for a closeness that was perfect. Still, in the back of her mind, Libby wondered if the tenderness would vanish with the guest.

"Now," Will announced with a flourish, "You two sit here on the floor in front of the tree." He led Libby to the center spot, dipped his arm indicating where she should sit, and placed the boy next to her, motioning to him to also sit. "And I shall prepare an exceptionally difficult meal in a matter of minutes."

"Oh, Will," Libby started to her feet. "You know when you get in the kitchen it takes weeks to get it organized again."

"Not this time, lady. And besides," he said in a tone a little sharper than he normally ever used, "why can't we have a messed-up kitchen once in a while? Makes the place feel like home."

A messed-up kitchen, like the one Will's mother had, a kitchen that was always sending wonderful smells out the kitchen window, not like the kitchen at her house. The take-out food, TV dinners, and cold cuts her mother brought home didn't smell like home. Libby didn't answer. Maybe Will was right.

She was too tired and unsettled to focus on the man she'd married, the man who was fussing over a little boy he'd brought home the same way he'd brought home birds with broken wings and lost pups when he was a child. Except this time Libby wasn't standing at his side ready to help.

FOUR

Libby leaned back watching as Will switched on the stereo and the record of Christmas carols she had been listening to the night of the famous plastic-wrap seduction. The child sat mesmerized at the blinking lights. Will was running the microwave in the kitchen and Libby began to think about what Will had said. Perhaps she was too organized, too neat, even if she had pitched her cape on the floor last night, where it would still be if Will hadn't hung it up for her.

Will never complained. Will never really said much of anything. He never had. Even when she had first come to Atlanta to business school, he'd never seemed to notice the way she'd moved into his life and reorganized it. She never knew that he was uncomfortable with her efforts. Today had been like the days they'd spent together when they were kids. Today they'd shared. She didn't even mind sharing him with Tiger.

"Libby! Hey, Lib!" Will's voice startled her back to the present and she looked up to see him standing before her with a tray filled with plastic cartons, paper plates, and napkins. He had pulled the trunk they used as a coffee table close by and was laying out his surprise. Such a hodge-podge of food might never find itself on the same table again. He'd bought sliced roast beef, ham, boiled shrimp, salads, bread, pickles, and a plastic bag of assorted cookies for desert. Tiger gave a cry of delight and sniffed the mixture of odors with the same exaggerated motions that Will had used the night before, enticing him to eat.

"No doubt about it," Will teased as he folded himself into an x and sat beside them, ladling full helpings of everything on their plates, "we've created a monster."

"I think you're right," Libby admitted, forcing herself to close out the memories and fall into the spirit of the occasion.

"What about this," Will exclaimed jovially, "let's make this a tradition. From now on, we decorate the Christmas tree and finish our work by enjoying its beauty as we partake of a smorgasbord fit for a king from the Delicious Deli."

"You're a nut," Libby sighed. "I've never heard you go on so. Come to think of it," she added seriously, "I've never heard you go on at all. This is a new Will Spencer. One I like very much." She looked at him, sure that the emotion she had felt all day was evident in her eyes and he returned her gaze, winking as he indicated by inclining his head that she should look at the child. Tiger's head was lolling dangerously as his eyes were almost closed.

"I'll give him a bath and put him to bed, Lib, while you clean up."

"I think I'll just leave the mess till morning," she said with a wicked tone. "Makes a house feel more homey, don't you think?" She rose to her feet and moved toward their bedroom, adding at the expression of surprise that washed across his face, "Why don't you save his bath till morning and bathe me instead?" Will's eyes opened in astonishment as Libby pulled her sweater over her head and left the room.

There was a definite lilt to Libby's walk as she flew to the bedroom. Humming with excited pleasure, she fumbled through her chest for the filmy red nightgown Dixie had sent for her last birthday. Next, she located a bottle of scented bubble bath and the fluffy oversized towels that she'd saved for a special occasion.

She turned and surveyed the bedroom. Too bright, she decided. All the lights must go, except the tiny bedside lamp. The quilted comforter had to be turned back, allowing crisp white sheets to show. When she was satisfied, she took off her clothes and put them away.

Libby energetically unbraided and began to brush her hair, impatient now for Will to join her. The memory of the intimacy of his gaze lingered in her mind and she knew the flush in her face was more enhancing than any make-up. When she was satisfied with her hair, she brushed her teeth, turned the radio to a station that played romantic music and sat on the edge of the bed to wait.

Her nervousness grew as the minutes passed and she began to fidget. She wanted the night to be like those romantic interludes she longed for. But the room was chilly and she was nude and she began to get very unromantic goosebumps. Finally, she wrapped her old robe around her and tiptoed down the hallway, peeping carefully into the small bedroom where Will lay, arm curled protectively around the boy, both sound asleep.

Shock, followed quickly by dismay that turned to anger, showered over her like white-hot rain. She stood in the doorway, a thousand hurting words roared through her mind, falling mute on lips trembling with the promise of tears. She whirled around and without a glance at the dinner remains, or the still twinkling tree, she threw the red nightgown, the toothbrush and comb in an overnight bag and buttoned her wool cape over her housecoat.

In a haze of tears she stuck her feet into shoes she didn't even see, slipped her purse under her arm, and started down the hall. When she passed the open doorway where Will and the child lay, she paused, pulled the door closed and leaned against it for a moment, telling herself that Will didn't deserve her anger. He wasn't doing anything that she hadn't done the night before. She shouldn't be so hurt.

But she was. She might be a rotten, selfish, uncaring person, but she was also hurt.

"I wanted you to be with me," she said as she stepped out into a foggy rain-soaked night. "But I guess that child can give you something I can't."

Will was never going to change. The great romance she'd envisioned as a sixteen-year-old never quite developed, even after she'd followed Will to Atlanta seven years ago. Though he'd willingly dropped by her first apartment several nights a week for dinner and to study in peace and quiet away from the noise of his dorm. They had quickly been accepted as a pair and included occasionally in parties and campus activities. But at the end of two years they were no closer than friends and Libby had finally accepted the fact that all the romance and passion were in her mind.

From medical school Will went on to take his residency at the county hospital under Emory's control. He was totally immersed in learning what made the body operate. By the time Libby graduated from business school, Will was specializing in orthopedic surgery and seriously studying computer science and design engineering at Georgia Tech. Left to her own devices, Libby found that she actually enjoyed her independence and her job.

As she drove through the rainy night, it all came back to her in a rush and, for a moment, she felt the same kind of loneliness that she'd felt back then when the relationship had almost ended. She and Will were on trains going in different directions, maybe they still were. She remembered the night she'd reached the end of her patience and gave Will an ultimatum.

"Will, I'm sorry," she'd said primly. "But if you don't marry me, I don't want to see you anymore." He had been munching on an apple, reading a text-book intently while she stared at the provocative cover of a new romance novel she'd been trying to read for the last hour. Her real life had reached the point that she could no longer identify with the heroine. All the book heroes were passionately attracted to their heroines, and you knew that sooner or later they would resolve their problems.

Libby and Will were an accepted pair, but what the world didn't know, and wouldn't have believed, was that they weren't lovers. They were more like friends, not even best friends at that, because best friends told each other all their deepest dreams, shared their problems and needs. The only things she shared with Will were pastrami sandwiches and washing powders.

He'd looked up at her, disbelief across his face. "What did you say?"

"I said, I don't want to see you anymore."

He pulled long legs beneath him and sat up, flicking the book closed with a crack of sound. "What did I do, Lib?"

"It isn't what you did, Will, it's more what you didn't, or don't do. I . . . I want a deeper relationship than you, with marriage and children and," she paused, embarrassed yet determined to say it all, ". . . making love."

She forced her gaze away from him, knowing that she wouldn't be able to say what she had made up her mind to say if she looked at the bewildered expression on his face. She'd give in and apologize. She looked at the floor.

"But, Lib. You know I like you. Hell, I mean, I probably even love you, but right now, with my residency and working toward my engineering degree . . . I mean . . ." he trailed off helplessly, as the unexpected confrontation threw him into an unfamiliar state of confusion.

"Do you realize, Will Spencer, that the few friends we have actually believe we're sleeping together, and you never even kiss me. I mean not a real honest-to-god, passionate body-touching kiss, not since I moved to Atlanta. We went further in high school than we do now. Don't you care about that anymore?"

"It isn't that I haven't thought about it," Will explained carefully, thinking out the words, "I have—a lot. But kissing seems to be the first step in a natural progression of events that I simply don't have time for, not now, not yet. It wouldn't be fair to you."

"I know, Will." The finality of his tone said more than his words.

"It will only be another two years, Libby, then I'll be ready to go into practice, then . . ."

"No, Will," Libby interrupted. "You just don't understand. These are the nineties—not the fifties. I want you to make love to me. I've waited for you since I was six years old. There's never been another man and I'm tired of just *reading* about sex and lovemaking." She stood up, threw the romance paperback across the room, and started unbuttoning her blouse.

Will had watched spellbound as she unbuttoned her blouse and unzipped the matching skirt, letting them fall silently to the floor. She could still remember the churning of her breath and the chattering of her teeth as he watched. She hadn't known what he would do when she unsnapped her bra and stood defiantly before him. But when he rose shakily and began to back away, she'd known she'd lost.

"I'm sorry, Libby," he'd choked. "But I can't . . . I have to think, I mean . . ."

And then he'd gone and the next weekend at Snow Lodge she met Stephen Colter, who had offered her the passion she'd wanted from Will.

She'd been the one to run away that time, retreating to her apartment, frantic with worry that after sleeping with Stephen Colter she might have gotten pregnant, that no man would ever want her, or that every man would want her and she wouldn't be able to say no.

It was the next week, after midnight, when her doorbell rang, a series of quick, sharp jabs that scared the life out of her. She was almost relieved when the knock came. The worst had happened, whatever the worst was. Will or Stephen, she didn't know who she wanted it to be. She put on her housecoat and turned on the hall light.

Through the peephole she saw Will, a very disheveled and uncoordinated Will, looking distinctly uncertain of himself. She opened the door and helped him inside. The smell of alcohol was almost overpowering.

"Libby," he said very slowly, spreading his long legs to steady himself. "I'll marry you. I'm here to make mad and passionate love to you." He gulped, gave a silly grin, and slid limply to the floor, sprawling his arms and legs like pick-up sticks. She couldn't believe it. Will Spencer had passed out cold.

Will Spencer, who didn't drink, had drunk enough

courage to come back to make love to Libby. She didn't know whether to laugh or cry.

"Damn you, Will Spencer." She'd stamped her foot in sheer frustration, looking at him slumped against the couch. "What am I supposed to do now? Take you back and go on like before, with you in one place and me in another? I can't do it. You may never get up this much courage again." She paced back and forth in futile recriminations. "Well, I can't get you up," she said in a huff, "so you'll just have to sleep where you are . . . unless . . ."

To this day she didn't know what made her do what she did. Her face burned even now as she remembered. She'd taken the pillows from her bed and the quilted comforter and laid them on the carpet. Next, she removed Will's sweatshirt. He'd been completely limp in her arms. She could do whatever she wanted. The sweatpants had been the hardest. Fingers stiff from nerves refused to cooperate, to untie the unyielding knot in the drawstring. Finally, she managed to loosen the knot and pulled the pants down.

She'd been glad that Will couldn't see her face when she looked down at the white jockey underwear revealing the bulge that signaled the obvious signs of his intent. She didn't know that men were *that way* when they were asleep, but Will was.

Quickly, she'd undressed and lay down stiffly beside him, almost bolting when he groaned and turned into her, throwing his leg possessively across her body. When he began to snore, she'd wanted to laugh. Nobody would believe this. It seemed like hours before she could still her breathing and force her body to relax. Once she'd thought out her plan, she surprised herself by going to sleep.

She thought it was the hard floor that woke her as the pale light of day turned the darkness of her tiny living room to a haze of smoky shapes.

Will was awake. She'd felt it in the frozen stiffness of the chest her head was resting on. There was an erotic beat to his heart and she could feel it pounding under her ear. She'd tried not to move, but her body seemed alive with the tingling of raw nerve endings and its subtle movement had overridden her normal control. When his hand reached out and tentatively closed around her breast, she'd almost groaned with desire.

Libby shivered. Will stopped. He released his fingers slowly and slid them away, leaving her suddenly exposed and cold. She'd moved closer until she felt hesitant fingers gain courage and encircle her nipple again. His touch spoke of uncertainty and a primitive agony shot through her with the heat of a raging broom sage fire in the fall. Then she, too, was touching, seeking, urging him to lift himself over her while her legs opened and lunged up to meet him.

"Libby, are you sure?" Will had whispered raggedly.

"You can't stop now," Libby answered hoarsely. "Please, Will. Please," she'd added in final desperation. "You didn't last night."

"Last night?"

"Last night when you made love to me."

"I did?" He'd moved over her. There was a roar at their coming together and it built and grew and rose with every thrust until she heard him cry out. He trembled, gave one final thrust and grew still.

It was Libby's body that continued to scream and jerk like an eddy in a stream.

"Oh, Libby," Will said with a wonder in his voice. "Oh, Libby, you were right. I never knew that it would be like that or we wouldn't have waited." Then, almost as an after thought, he'd said, "I'm sorry about coming here like I did, drinking. I mean drunk, forcing myself on you. You know, I must have passed out. I don't remember last night being so good."

"But it was, Will, and it'll just get better and better—I mean that's what everyone says."

They'd moved in together the next week, but somehow the getting better hadn't quite worked out like "they said." At first, she justified her dissatisfaction by saying that Stephen had been an experienced lover. That once Will learned, she would feel what he was feeling. Then, she decided that something was wrong with her. Will loved her. She loved Will. That ought to make everything right—but it didn't.

Finally, Libby faced the truth; the only place she felt butterflies and sky rockets was in her romance novels—until Stephen Colter came back into her life.

When Libby rang Dixie Lee Kendall's doorbell an hour later, she was completely drained, soaking wet, and limp from emotional exhaustion.

"Good Lord, Libby, have you been hitchhiking?" Dixie was wearing a gold satin hostess pajama outfit and an Egyptian headpiece as casually as a sweatband and a jogging suit.

Libby opened her mouth, prepared to tell Dixie about what had happened, and choked back a sob instead. "Oh, Dixie, I think I've run away from home. May I come in?"

"What do you mean?" demanded Dixie, sweeping Libby inside, ignoring the small group of startled guests in the process of donning coats and wraps to leave. "Of course, you can come in. Let's go upstairs and you can tell me what's wrong."

Dixie led her up the stairs and into the pink little-girl bedroom she'd abandoned when her father had decorated a suite of rooms for her on her eighteenth birthday. She placed her hands on Libby's shoulders and marched her stiffly to the bed. "What's wrong, Libby? I've never seen you lose control before."

"Dixie, I've left Will. I mean he fell asleep and then I was waiting for him to bathe me and he never came and I already had bubble bath and my red nightgown and I didn't even clean up the shrimp for once."

"Wait a minute. You're not making sense. If I didn't know better, I'd think that Libby Spencer was babbling. Stay here while I get you a glass of wine," Dixie said, glancing back at her when she reached the door, as if she were afraid to leave Libby alone.

"No wine, Dixie." Libby refused and sank wearily to the bed. "I'd probably eat the glass. I just want to sleep. I've never been so tired."

"Fine, let's get your wet cape off and . . ." Dixie turned back to Libby and prodded, half lifting her as she unbuttoned the soaked cape. Dixie shook her head in amusement at the sight of the frayed cotton housecoat beneath. "When you leave, you don't waste any time planning do you?"

"No, I just left."

"Okay, love, no more questions. Let me have that whatever it is you're wearing and you crawl in bed."

Libby unsnapped the top buttons, stopped suddenly, and began to giggle. "You're not going to believe this, Dixie, but I'm not wearing anything under this housecoat."

"Lord love a duck, when you flip out, you turn cartwheels. Miss Organization has come totally unglued. Here, sit down and calm yourself while I say good night to my guests. When I get back, we'll find you a nightgown."

The silence enclosed Libby after the slamming of the bedroom door, and all her sudden bravado died in the wake of realization. How could she have done such a dumb thing, leave her apartment and drive around half the night with no clothes on? She couldn't believe her actions. Pop would be shocked. Nice girls didn't do such immature things. He would have expected better of her. If Will hadn't responded like she'd expected him to, she must have done something wrong. It had to be her fault.

Maybe, she thought wearily, she ought to have thrown a screaming fit, beaten him up or something.

Libby's glance fell on the overnight case and the fluff of red inside, the sexy nightgown Dixie had given her. Libby heard herself giggle. The red nightgown caper had been as successful as the plastic wrap. As a femme fatale she was a complete washout. With a sigh, she discarded the housecoat, pulled on the nightgown, and crawled into bed, wet hair and all.

If Scarlett O'Hara could worry tomorrow, so could she. There must be an answer, a way to force Will to see her as a woman, with physical needs. Just let him worry about her for a change, she thought sleepily as the tenseness began to subside. Just this once, Libby Spencer would forget to come home.

"Libby, Libby, wake up! There's a telephone call for you." Someone was shaking her shoulder insistently, "Libby! Will's on the phone. I think you'd better answer."

"Will?" Libby opened her eyes to see Dixie's concerned face above hers. "Dixie? Oh." It all came back in a rush. She'd come to Dixie's last night, after . . . "How'd he find me?"

"I don't know, but it's afternoon and he sounds very concerned." Dixie spoke soothingly, nodding at the pink phone on the table beside the bed. She opened the drapes to reveal a dark, closed-in day, an extension of the weather Libby had driven around in last night.

"I've brought you something to wear, at least I think Monica's about your size."

"Monica?" Libby repeated stupidly, moistening her lips, in dread of the confrontation with Will.

"One of the maids," Dixie explained as she left the room. "You're not superman, you can't run around in broad daylight with nothing on but a red cape and sneakers, even if it is foggy outside. Now, answer that phone before I'm arrested for kidnapping, then come down to lunch."

Libby took a deep breath and picked up the pink telephone. "Hello?"

"Libby, are you okay?"

Libby hadn't known what to expect, but the controlled concern she heard now came as a surprise. "No," she admitted and slid to a sitting position, pulling the sheet along with her. "No, I'm not all right, I seem to be coming unglued and I don't know why." She heard the tremor in her voice and pressed her lips together.

"Maybe I do," he said softly. "Maybe I don't blame you."

"You don't? Well I do. Neither your parents, nor mine, at least Pop, would ever have run away from home, no matter what. If you have a problem, you're supposed to face up to it. I just don't think I like our life very much and I don't know what went wrong, or what to do to make it right."

"Come home, Lib, and we'll talk about it."

"We will?" She wanted to think that they would, but she knew that would be difficult under the best of conditions. With a guest, even a child, talking would be impossible. "We can't," she finally said. "We have company, maybe later, after . . ."

"No. Tiger has to go back to the hospital tomorrow for tests and measurements. He won't be here with us again until next weekend, and he doesn't have to come then, if you'd rather not."

"The next weekend, Christmas? We're taking him to your folks for Christmas?" Libby's voice was too loud, but she couldn't conceal her dismay. "Will, I'm so sorry. I don't mean to be selfish. I sound like some terrible, awful shrew and I can't seem to stop myself.''

"It's okay, Lib, I want you to be honest with me for a change. We'll do whatever you say, but I just didn't want the little fella to spend Christmas in the hospital even if he doesn't know about Santa Claus.''

Honest with him? Libby was always honest. At least she thought she had been. Trouble was, they'd had so little time together there was nothing to be honest about.

"It's just that he's so alone,'' Will said softly.

There was a wistfulness in Will's voice that Libby couldn't ignore. She did understand, but somehow it didn't make things right. Her silence echoed in her ear and Will finally spoke again.

"Maybe this is better, Libby. Take a few days and we'll both think things over, then come home and we'll talk.''

After she hung up the phone, Libby sat, thinking about what they'd said. She wondered if Will had cleaned away the mess in the living room. It had always been important to her that her house be immaculate. She wanted everything to be just right. Her motivation was obvious, even to her mother.

Alice McHanie never wanted to grow old. She fought it every step of the way; even had her only child call her by her first name. Alice had been a careless housekeeper, preferring to spend her time with more fulfilling things, like the theater, politics, and her tennis club. Anything, Libby always thought, except her and Pop. Even to a child it had been painfully obvious that her mother and father were mismatched. Alice had been a whirlwind of activity, looking for excitement, friends, and something Libby never quite understood.

Pop, well Pop had been special. He had adored Libby, allowing her total freedom as long as she conducted herself properly. He hadn't seemed to mind being given orders, caring for Libby alone, even doing much of the housework.

When Alice McHanie had suffered a sudden paralyzing stroke, she'd retired bitterly to a nursing home. "I'm not staying around where anyone can see me like this," she'd insisted.

"But, Mother, I don't want you to go." Libby had cried then. Alice died two years later and Libby hadn't cried anymore. It had always been her and Pop and her mother's absence was something she hardly noticed at all. During her first year at the bank, Pop had died and then she realized how lonely he must have been. She'd vowed then that she would be a perfect wife, keep her house spotless and put the man she loved first. Why weren't things working out? As she got out of bed, she chastised herself for thinking of Stephen Colter. She'd never thought she was at all like Alice—until now.

The borrowed slacks and sweater fit perfectly and went reasonably well with the still-damp sneakers she'd worn last night. She found a brush in her overnight bag and untangled her hair, leaving it hanging loose to her shoulders. She was pale, dark eyes staring hollowly out of a face that was pinched and drawn. Shakily, she added lipstick, then decided it made her look garish and wiped it off again, leaving only the pale tint.

As she followed the white-spindled staircase

downstairs, she thought about how she must have looked last night when Dixie opened the door. Wet hair, plastered down, pink-winged jogging shoes and a housecoat hanging down beneath her cape. She grinned and shook her head as the smell of coffee led her to a bright, cheerful breakfast room where Dixie was reading the newspaper and smoking a cigarette.

"I thought you'd quit smoking," Libby commented.

"I've been found out. Come and have some coffee and pretend you didn't see me."

"What do you mean?" Libby took a cup from the antique buffet, filled it with coffee, added both cream and sugar, and sat down across from Dixie.

"I never really stopped completely. I lie about it. That's the way I keep it under control. That's only one of my little games, my public image."

"Lie?" Her mind flew back to Will's words. *I wish you would be completely honest with me.* "That's what Will said, that I'm not honest."

"Who is, love? We all see what we want to see and improvise or twist the rest to fit, you more so than most. You have your life with Will all planned out. When your relationship didn't go the way you planned, you just refused to see it."

"But I didn't want it to be like . . . I mean, I planned everything to be perfect, but Will's more interested in his career than he is in me. I mean, he actually brought home a child and you should have seen him . . ." And before she realized it, she'd told Dixie the whole thing. "And then he took the child to bed and fell asleep. There I was, waiting like a naked fool in the bedroom with bubble bath in one hand and my red nightgown in the other.''

"Libby," Dixie said softly, blowing a steady puff of silver smoke across the room, "the child is a part of the thing Will is most interested in—his work. And he needs Will.''

"What do you mean? I need Will, too.''

"For what?''

"To be interested in me," she stammered. "To care about me, make love to me," she finished lamely.

Dixie stubbed out the cigarette, looked at Libby's now-cold cup of coffee, shoved it aside, and poured another. "Drink and listen. Think about what you said. You need him to be interested in you, care about you, and make love to you. Let's start with the first, interested in you. Are you interested in him?''

"Of course, I am, Dixie," Libby flashed, dropping the cup into its saucer with a rattle. "You know I am.''

"All right, what does Will actually do? What is he doing with that child?''

"He works with computers and he makes artificial limbs. He and his friend Pat are developing some new heart valve. The little boy is scheduled for an artificial arm, I think. I'm not really sure of the details. He doesn't discuss all that technical stuff with me.''

"Do you ask?''

"Well, no. I don't understand what he's talking about half the time. I guess the way it worked out is that he has his work and I have mine.''

"Libby, I happen to know how much time you

spend with your elderly bank customers and with the people in your neighborhood who need your services, but if I do say so, you've been pretty tunnel-visioned when it comes to Will's interests. He isn't just a husband, he's a man with deep commitment, too. I'm wondering if he has the same feelings about your interests as you do about his?''

"But I do care, Dixie. Why are you twisting things? Will doesn't ask about my work either. He doesn't even care that they're about to merge my bank into that monster chain.''

"Have you told him?''

"No, but he should have asked.''

"I know Will is a genius, but I don't think even he would know to ask about something he doesn't know about.''

"Oh, stop it, Dixie. The important thing is that I love Will. I always have. You know that.''

"I know, kid,'' Dixie said softly. "You've always loved Will. I admire that, but I'm not sure it's the honest truth. Do you really love Will Spencer, or have you created a Will Spencer in your mind that you love and suddenly the real thing isn't measuring up?''

This wasn't what she expected from Dixie. Dixie had always been on her side. Now, she was just confusing her. Libby felt great hot tears roll down her face and she began to cry silently. Dixie simply handed her a napkin and let her cry. "I don't understand, Dixie. What makes you so smart? You sound like Pop.''

"I'm not so smart, Libby. I'm just a parrot, repeating all those things I read, and I care about you.'' She inclined her head toward the bookcase surrounding the door at the other end of the room where Libby saw shelves and shelves of books and dog-eared manuals.''

''You've read all these?''

''Yes. I really did get a degree. I was training to be a psychologist, but Daddy wouldn't hear of it. And to tell the truth, I'm too lazy to go on and get all those other degrees that make you respectable. So, I volunteer.''

''Where?''

''The family crisis center. Now, don't you go and tell anyone and blow my image. That's why I got my hair spiked. It makes the kids identify with me.''

Too many things were coming at Libby for her to comprehend. Dixie as a counselor?

''Why don't you stay here for a day or two, Libby, and think things over and we'll see if we can come up with an idea or two.''

''That's what Will suggested. But I don't have any clothes and I have to go to work tomorrow and meet the transition committee. I can't wear a housecoat.''

''Fine, we have all this afternoon to shop. You know,'' Dixie mused with a glint in her eye. ''Maybe I was wrong the other day at lunch. You're the one who needs shaking up. Maybe if you thought Will was having an affair you'd do something to make him notice you, starting with some clothes that don't look like early menopause.''

When Dixie paused before the store window display of ballgowns and evening wear, Libby stopped, too, dutifully adding her own comments of admiration.

"Let's get that slinky red one for you, Libby?"

"Good heavens. What for? I'll never go anywhere I can wear that. We couldn't afford it."

"Why ever not? Will has a good job. You have a good job. Why not?"

"Well, number one, where would I wear it? We really don't have any friends to speak of. The closest Will comes to nightlife is his jog in the park."

"Surely, you'll be invited out over the holidays?"

"I doubt it. I mean Will has Pat and his cronies from the lab, and I have the girls from the office and some of what Will calls my little old ladies. And the truth is, I hate to spend money foolishly when Will seems to need our extra money for his research."

"But I thought the university paid for all that?"

"Not unless it's something they have a grant or a contract for. This new computer arm they're trying to develop is Will's own project, and boy do those bills add up."

"I see," Dixie commented, glancing once more at the dress and moving down the mall. She was getting that look on her face again and Libby was afraid that meant she was off again. But she didn't say anything and Libby began to relax.

By the time they headed back to the car, Libby had given up and the arms of both girls were filled with packages: shoes, dresses, underwear. Libby didn't want to think how much she'd spent on herself. In three hour's time, she had bought clothes she never would have even tried on if Dixie hadn't been along. She was surprised at herself and how out-of-character she'd behaved.

Now, suddenly, she began to worry. She ought to

go home. She wanted to go home, but what would she say to Will? What would he say to her? She wished he was a traveling salesman and had to leave for the week. She needed time to work things out in her mind about her and Will, and about the bank, and about the person she tried to keep herself from thinking about—Stephen Colter.

"What now, love?" It was as if Dixie had followed her train of thought.

They carried the packages up to the bedroom and dropped them on the perfectly-made bed. "I don't know," Libby admitted. "I just don't know. If it weren't for the problem of the bank merger, I would feel better. I mean, Will and I are having all this trouble, it's Christmas, we have a strange child in the house, and now—the bank."

What Libby couldn't say or confess was her meeting with Stephen. She didn't know whether she was keeping a secret because she was ashamed, or because it was special and private.

"Well, I don't want to interfere, Lib, but perhaps you do need to take a little time and remake your plans. You're welcome to stay with me as long as you want. I have a dinner party tonight at the Hinkle's, you're welcome to come along."

"No thanks," Libby said quickly. The last thing she wanted was to go to a dinner party with Dixie. "Just let me stay here and think things out if I'm not in the way. Am I taking your bedroom?"

"Goodness, no. This was my little-girl room. I've grown up to something other than pink and ruffles. Daddy is just sentimental about it. You know, now that I think about it, this is just what I mean. This room looks like you, innocent and sweet. Think about that and your apartment, Lib.''

Libby looked around after Dixie left. Dixie had been right. Libby did feel comfortable in this room. She thought about her bedroom at home, the one she shared with Will. It wasn't pink or ruffled. It was colorless. She and Will had lived together for three years, but it was as if the room were still waiting to be stamped with their imprint. Unfinished. Other than the schefflera tree and a couple of colored pillows on the bed, the decor of the room reflected neither of them.

The rest of their apartment was done in shades of blues and greens, cool and restrained. She didn't know what Will's office looked like. You couldn't see the walls and furniture for the equipment and reference materials. Her image at the bank was tailored and efficient. She addressed all her clients by their last name and she never referred to herself as Ms. If that made her out-of-step, she supposed there was nothing she could do about that.

If Will didn't like her image, she would change it. If he'd tell her what he wanted. She could change the apartment, too, if—it occurred to her that she didn't know what Will thought about their apartment. When she'd moved in, she'd quietly put a woman's touch on the apartment and he'd never said a word. He'd never seemed to mind. He never seemed to notice.

Libby unpacked the clothes she and Dixie had bought. What on earth possessed her to buy a short black leather skirt and a pale lavender bulky knit sweater to wear with it? Nobody at the bank wore black hose and boots. She could imagine what Miss Lois and the other ladies at the retirement home would say if she was wearing boots and leather when she came over to take them shopping. She wondered what Will would think.

Everything always came back to Will and what he'd think. She and Will had seemed so right in the beginning. They'd be married, he'd become a doctor, and they'd have two children. But Will hadn't practiced medicine and she'd become involved at the bank, and the wedding had been squeezed in between conferences and work schedules. The children had been delayed without ever being discussed.

What had happened? Why had they drifted so far apart? Why hadn't it stayed simple? Will was brilliant. Why didn't he understand how she was feeling? Stephan did. Stephen Colter. He always seemed to appear in her life just when she was at a crisis point.

Everything went round and round in her mind until she couldn't think about it any longer. She cleared away the shopping bags, put on her red nightgown, and crawled between the sheets. When the phone rang, she didn't answer it. She knew it was Will and she didn't know what to say.

"Sorry I'm late, Mr. Marvin. I had to stop by the apartment complex and pick up the checks for some of our clients."

"I just don't feel right about you carrying that much money back to them, alone. I don't know what the merger is going to do to your little courier service to the old folks home."

"I know," she agreed sadly, glancing at her watch. Normally, she arrived much earlier. But coming from Dixie's had thrown her timetable off. "I've been worrying about that, too, but I just can't believe that anyone in headquarters really cares what we do down here."

The morning passed unusually slowly, giving Libby far too much time to dwell on a solution to her problem. She kept remembering Dixie's questions. Maybe she ought to take a greater interest in Will's projects. Maybe she ought to force Will to sit down and listen to her's. But it wasn't talking that she missed. It was touching and being touched. It was feeling special.

Libby was sitting at her desk going around in circles when Lewis Marvin approached her.

"Libby, why don't you go on to lunch and then report to the main office downtown this afternoon. They've asked to have you reassigned to assist the transition officer in making recommendations and submitting information to the board of directors during the merger."

"Me? Why? Did you recommend me?"

"No. I would have if they'd asked. The message just came from Mrs. Hadley."

"Mr. Marvin, you know that the last thing I want to do is help merge Peachtree National out of existence. Can't you get me out of it?"

"Look at it this way, Libby. Maybe it's our best chance to keep things like we want. With you to sell our old personal approach, we stand a better chance of keeping things as they are."

"All right," she agreed reluctantly. "But I don't intend to be some mealy-mouthed yes-man, eh woman. I'm going to have my say. I don't understand why they chose me." She gathered up the things she needed from her desk and looked around the banking floor with a sense of doom. For all she knew, this might be her last time to walk across the polished wood floors and look up at the high ceilings and brass rails.

At the door, she turned back to the trailing Mr. Marvin. "Will you take the money over to the complex? Just go to Miss Lois Nettles's apartment on the ground level. She'll get you to the others. I meant to tell them about the merger myself, but it looks like I might not get there today."

Libby spent a troubled lunch hour at a diner near the main office downtown. Stopping by the ladies' room, she glanced in the mirror and regretted ever allowing herself to follow Dixie's buying suggestions. She was wearing one of the more subdued dresses, a black scooped necked knit with a wide camel colored strip along the permanently pleated skirt. Black opaque hose, medium-heeled black pumps, and a heavy, smooth gold necklace and earrings completed the picture. Her hair was pinned up in its usual chignon and her makeup still seemed smooth and businesslike, except for the flush of anger that had given a healthy glow to her cheeks.

"Good afternoon, Mrs. Spencer." Mrs. Hadley, Mr. Todd's assistant, greeted her with a look that said very well what she thought of Libby's appointment to the transition committee. "I hope you understand that we expect you to represent Peachtree National with dedication and a professional attitude."

Libby took a deep breath. If she was going to be able to help the branches, she had to speak out and stand her ground, beginning now. "Mrs. Hadley, I intend to represent the branch banks as honestly as I know how, but I don't intend to be a figurehead or a yes-man. Where is the V.I.P. I've been assigned to?"

A thin frown narrowed Mrs. Hadley's lips as she indicated, with an outstretched hand, the door at the end of the hall. Libby felt the woman's eyes bore through her like pinpoints of hot sunlight as she walked down the hallway.

So, you put Mrs. Hadley in her place, Libby thought. What makes you think that the transition committee will let you get away with opening your mouth? And even if they do, they're unlikely to listen to what you have to say. Be firm, she directed herself. Pretend he is Will and you're telling him why you were unhappy about being left on the street corner in the cold. That's it, she decided as she poised outside the door, extended her hand to knock, then shrugged her shoulders and went in, ready to make her position clear from the beginning.

The man behind the desk had his back to her, speaking briskly in the telephone for a moment before swinging around. Beginning at the floor in front of her feet, his gaze traveled up her body until he reached the dawning of recognition in her eyes.

"Stephen."

"So, it is you. I could only hope that the twenty-seven-year-old assistant branch manager named Libby, with the business school background, was you."

"You actually sent for me?"

"Not exactly. The computer threw out several logical prospects that might be acceptable to the old employees as a representative to the committee. I simply noticed the coincidence and hoped. Why'd you run away again, Libby?"

The floor seemed to shift. She felt as if she was standing on a waterbed, and she knew that unless she sat down she was likely to start her great attack from a very unprofessional position. She couldn't seem to find words as she put one foot gingerly in front of the other until she reached the back of the tall leather chair to the side of the oversize walnut desk where Stephen Colter was sitting.

I can't let him know how he affects me, she kept telling herself. This is business. I must get control, otherwise I will lose any hope of saving the bank, and myself as well, she admitted. With visible straightening of her shoulders, Libby cleared her throat and walked casually around the chair and sat down, crossing her legs with deliberate slowness.

"Hello, Stephen. I should have figured out that you were the transition officer. Nobody conducts out-of-town business the week before Christmas except a man on his way to making a million dollars." She began to relax, the crisp light tone was just right and Stephen leaned back, eyes narrowing in speculation as she continued. "So, now we work together. Are you sure you want to, Stephen? I warn you. I'm dead set against changing the way our branch banks operate."

"Can we work together? I don't know, about the work, that is. The together sounds like a challenge, and I'm willing to take my chance on the work. You see, Libby, in spite of what has happened, you come very highly recommended. The board of directors likes the reputation you have of answering customers' needs. We want to use it, and you, to make the community take the merger with the best possible enthusiasm."

"Are you really open to suggestions, or do you want me to do the dirty work?"

"You've changed, Libby. You're much more in control, mature than you were six years ago. I think

I like the new Libby. I'm even more intrigued by this one than the other.''

"Stephen, this is a business office and this conference is taking place during business hours, therefore I suggest we get back to business." Libby forced herself to face Stephen's amused expression without flinching. He knew that her words were an attempt to direct his attention away from what had happened in the past and he knew that she was aware of his knowledge. He only smiled for a moment, then agreed with a tilt of his head.

"So, I'm faced with the prototype of the modern American working woman. Direct, to the point, and all business—no fooling around with the boss on her way to the top. And, make no mistake, Libby, simply by acting as my assistant in the merger, you are on the way. Where you stop will depend entirely on you.''

Stephen was interrupted by the ring of the phone and Libby breathed a sigh of relief. How much longer she could have carried out the pose he had just described was a question she didn't want to consider. There was a knot in the pit of her stomach that was only a little smaller than the one in her throat. Watching the tall, bearded man with the deep blue eyes as he spoke on the phone made it clear that a firm business relationship was the only defense she had against being swept up in what his words had offered. As he hung up the phone, she made a last attempt to set up a barrier between them.

"Stephen, I'm married. I told you that before. My marriage,'' she faltered and knew the faltering gave her away, ''may not be the strongest in the world, but it's mine and I don't intend to do anything to end it.''

"All right, Libby. Don't panic. Right now, all we have to do is begin the proposals and reports that the executive committee will need to decide what changes will be made. I'd like you to compile a list of personnel who would make good company people, a list of personnel ready for retirement or with questionable efficiency ratings, and a third list of obvious unsuitables. From these lists management will determine which of our people will be transferred in, and which of yours will be sent to the home office for training. Can you do that, Mrs. Spencer?''

"Certainly, Mr. Colter. But my main concern lies in what plans you have for our branch banks and those customers. Will I be able to offer a proposal in that respect?''

"By all means,'' he answered, his voice even, his eyes staring at her as if he were a cat and she were the goldfish inside the bowl. "You will have the adjacent office. Select a secretary who is efficient and can keep her mouth shut.''

"What about Mrs. Hadley?''

Stephen smiled. "You mean the dragon lady? Suit yourself, but I think you're inviting the voice of doom into our negotiations.''

"Certainly I'm not her greatest fan, but she is intensely loyal and devoted to the bank. She will defend our position to the death and we just might win her over.''

"Suit yourself,'' he agreed with a laugh. "But I'm inclined to believe it's more likely *our* death.''

"When shall I begin?'' Libby stood, grateful to

find that her feet seemed to have found their sea legs, that or the floor had stopped moving.

"Right now. Start with these records and computer printouts. Match them up according to personality profiles, personnel records, instincts, whatever. Just get the list together."

For the rest of the afternoon Libby worked steadily, satisfied that although the Stephen/Libby issue wasn't settled, for now Stephen's need for a professional job overrode any personal relationship and he was surprisingly easy to work with. She could see why his superiors had selected him for the job.

While Mrs. Hadley had been suspicious and cagey at Libby's request for assistance, she, too, began to fit in and the list began to grow.

"Mrs. Spencer?" Mrs. Hadley was standing hesitantly in the doorway. "It's almost five. If you need me to stay on, I'll be glad to. And there's a Dixie Lee on the phone. I told her you weren't taking calls, but she insisted."

"I'll take the call, Mrs. Hadley, and please call me Libby. You needn't be so formal. I'm uncomfortable enough with being here." She picked up the phone, hesitated, and turned back to the ram-rod still woman in the doorway. "Thank you for offering to work late, but not tonight. I don't know what we're going to do next and I need time to get better organized. I'll see you in the morning."

"My, that sounded very professional, Libby. If I hadn't recognized your voice, I wouldn't have known it was you."

"Dixie, what on earth are you calling down here for? How did you find me?"

"Part bloodhound, girl. Some nice old gentleman in your office said you'd been sent downtown. Of course, I immediately thought he meant police headquarters. You didn't embezzle any money, did you?"

"Of course not. I've been assigned to assist the new liaison officer handling the merger. Why'd you call?"

"Oh, I almost forgot. Will called. Apparently they wouldn't tell him where you were and he was afraid you were leaving town, but you're getting me off track. That's not what I called for."

Leaving town? Surely, Will didn't think she'd go anywhere without talking to him, did he? "What did you call for Dixie? I'm really busy."

The office door between her office and Stephen's opened and she knew he was standing there listening. Her mouth went dry and she felt like a child with her hand caught in the cookie jar. Dixie couldn't see him, but if she had she would have immediately started off on some wild tangent Libby didn't want to think about.

"Oh, all right, Libby. I've been downtown, working out a surprise that will knock your socks off and I thought you might give me a ride home."

"Hold on just a moment." She put her hand over the phone and turned to Stephen. "Do you need me? This is personal, but I can cut it short."

"Well, yes. I wondered if you could stay downtown and have dinner with me. We could map out our plans for the next day or two, over a steak."

"Uh, no. I mean, that's what the phone call is about. I already have plans for the evening." She took her hand off the receiver and blurted out far too eagerly. "Of course, I'll meet you, just as we planned. When and where, darling?"

"Darling? As we planned? Well I can't wait to find out what this is about. I'll meet you in the lobby in fifteen minutes. I'm about a block away. And by the way, darling, tell whoever you're putting on this act for that I'm mad about you."

"Your husband?" Stephen's dry comment seemed more tinged with amusement than annoyance. "Well, never mind, another time will do just as well. Good night, Mrs. Spencer."

"All right, give. Who were you putting on the act for? The liaison officer? Your new boss? Let me guess, he's about forty . . ."

"Thirty-five," Libby supplied before she realized that she had spoken.

"Thirty-five," Dixie corrected, "tall, dark, and very persuasive."

"Blond and how'd you know he was persuasive?"

"Love, you wouldn't have provided an alibi unless you were in danger of needing one, now give. Tell Dixie all about him."

"Not on your life, Dixie Lee Kendall. You'll just go on a tangent and that's what I don't need right now. I have enough problems as it is. Besides, you haven't told me what you've been up to. I distinctly sense an aura of mystery about your afternoon. You first, give . . ."

And she did, and Libby's heart sank. If Dixie carried out her latest plan it ought to just about end their friendship as far as Will was concerned. Libby shuddered to think about what it would do to the relationship between her and Will. But as usual, when you were dealing with Dixie, you were the last to learn of her plans. Libby would just have to hope it worked out.

For the next few days Stephen neither said nor did anything to disrupt the work and they made remarkable progress. Libby began to believe that she just might like her trip to the top. The only cloud on the horizon was Will. She missed him, even if he didn't talk to her, even if he did sit up and read in bed every night instead of cuddling her in his arms. And she was worried. She'd hoped that he would come for her.

There were just two days left until Christmas Eve. Christmas was for families. And Will was her family. Libby couldn't stay with Dixie any longer. There was a nagging voice in the back of her mind that sounded like Pop's, telling her that it was time for her to go home.

It was Wednesday afternoon, the day before Christmas Eve, when she knocked on Stephen's office door.

"Come in."

"Stephen, may I leave early? Tomorrow is Christmas Eve and we close at noon. We've been so busy around here that I haven't finished my Christmas shopping. There is something I very much need to do."

"Of course, Libby. I'm leaving later tonight myself, flying to Connecticut for the holidays. As a matter-of-fact, I'd like to go shopping with you," he added. "I'd like to buy a gift for you and I want you to help me select it, for size."

"No," she refused sharply. "I can't. Besides, you don't need to buy a gift for me. The raise in my check this morning was far too generous and I know you were responsible. That's more than enough." She turned and quickly left the office, afraid that his suggestion was inviting a return of the awareness she had almost been able to forget.

"Merry Christmas, Libby," Stephen's voice called. "And I know you're going to have a Happy New Year. One way or the other, I'm going to see to it personally."

"I'll see to it personally."

Stephen's words vibrated in Libby's ears and she caught her breath as she realized what she was thinking. Suddenly she had to get away from the office, the overwhelming presence of this man who was a threat to her life with Will, if she was ever going to be able to erase the fantasy that was building in her mind.

The piped-in music in the elevator played Christmas carols nonstop, and when the elevator doors opened on the lobby floor she could see a Salvation Army worker ringing her bell outside the building, followed by the resounding echo of coins falling into the black iron tub.

As she pulled her little compact car out into the street, the traffic officer turned her in the opposite direction, down past Rich's Department Store with its enormous roof-top tree. Impulsively, she drove into the parking deck. It had been years since she'd shopped downtown, not since the first Christmas she and Will had been married when she had sat impishly on Santa's knee. She'd whispered in his ear that all she wanted for Christmas was a skinny little boy with bashful laughing eyes like the man leaning against the big icicle.

Laughing eyes. Until Tiger came how long had it been since she'd seen laughing eyes? Will was more often serious, or contemplative, or worried. Libby closed and locked her car and walked over the crosswalk to the store. The toy department was one floor up and Libby headed for the escalator. The store even smelled like Christmas and the merry Christmas sounds of the store bells and music made her feel ten years old. She stepped off the escalator and turned toward the toy department.

The Christmas shoppers were nearly done now and the aisles were strangely vacant. The toys lay in disarray, among empty boxes and vacant tables. A wind-up monkey with clapping cymbals caught her eye. Next to the monkey was a table of moving trains. She could almost see Will and the child on the floor putting the pieces together.

Will and the child. She shook herself, trying to push away the thought. But it was no use. Will had been right to bring Tiger home. She wouldn't want to leave a small boy in the hospital over Christmas, no matter what her and Will's problems were. She would go and get the child herself. Quickly, she purchased the monkey, a train set, several assorted picture books, anxious now to collect the child and get home to Will. On the way out, for some reason she couldn't explain, she bought a very small lifelike baby doll that cried when you cuddled it.

After she left the store, she went to the hospital.

She'd only been there once and that had been a long time ago. She didn't know where in the hospital Tiger would be. When she identified herself as Libby Spencer to the volunteer in the lobby, they knew her immediately and greeted her with enthusiasm.

"Of course, Mrs. Spencer. Tiger is up on five. Dr. Spencer told us he might take the boy home today. Your husband is such a fine man and so much fun to work with."

"Will, fun?" Libby could have imagined many things said about Will, but fun?

At every station she was greeted warmly. All the employees sounded Will's praises. By the time she reached Tiger's room and opened the door Libby had learned more about her husband's reputation as a humanitarian than she'd learned from Will in three years.

"Libby?" Tiger held out his arm and Libby quite naturally lifted him. He raised his solemn eyes and voiced the tentative, "Go?"

She nodded and sat him back on the edge of the bed as she began to gather his clothes. If anyone had asked, she wouldn't have been able to give a sensible explanation for her actions. She could only say that it was Christmas and this was a child who needed love at the time of year when love should be everyone's gift.

Tiger's growing vocabulary now included a very sing-song, creative version of "Jingle Bells" and much to his delight Libby joined in and they sang all the way back to the apartment. As she drove she worked out the details of Tiger's stay in her mind. If Will had to work in the morning, Libby would take Tiger with her. He could sit quietly in her office and play.

Or, better still, she'd leave him with Miss Lois. The old people would thoroughly enjoy a little one and she already felt guilty about not having been by to check on them since she'd been transferred downtown.

Then, after the bank closed at noon, they'd pack the car and drive to Will's folks for Christmas Eve. It would be fun playing Santa. Will would never fill out Pop's old red moth-eaten Santa suit, but maybe Mr. Spencer would play the part. Beyond that, she couldn't go.

Libby didn't know whether or not Will had done any grocery shopping while she'd been at Dixie's, and she was afraid to see what the apartment looked like. She decided that if she wanted to eat she'd better not take any chances. She pulled into the shopping center, lifted Tiger and placed him securely in a cart abandoned in the space next to her car. Inside the store, his eyes grew big as saucers as he took in all the aisles of food. When they reached the fruit section, he motioned frantically toward the bananas and began peeling one before Libby even had them weighed. "Never mind," the clerk said with good humor, "Merry Christmas, kid."

"Kid," that was what Will and Dixie called her. Maybe they were right. Maybe she was a kid. Certainly at Christmas she was. She wondered if Will had watered their tree. She'd missed their lovely Christmas tree while she'd been at Dixie's. The snow-flocked one in Dixie's hallway was artistically perfect, but Libby missed the lopsided decorations

Tiger had placed at the bottom of their tree. With a lilt in her step now, she hurriedly filled her basket and took Tiger and the groceries back to the car.

By the time they reached the apartment a fine mist had begun to fall, and they had to hurry to get the bags of groceries inside before the rain began. *I left when it was raining,* she thought, *and it rains now, like I haven't been away, but I have. I've been a very long way, and I don't know if I'm back yet.*

Will wasn't at home and Libby quickly began to put away her groceries. The apartment was absolutely clean, not a speck of dust, no loaf of bread on the counter, and no wet shirt on the schefflera tree. Even the Christmas tree stand had water. And the pink roses were gone. Will must have hired a maid. It certainly didn't look like he lived here. She thought with guilt of her own recent sloppy habits. Outside her own home she didn't have to be so perfect and she had become downright messy at Dixie's.

When Will gets home, a homemade chicken pie and yeast rolls will be cooking in the oven, Libby planned happily. She kept moving, activity and stubborn determination keeping Stephen Colter out of her thoughts.

I'll have Tiger bathed and will already be dressed in his pajamas. After a quiet dinner she'd put Tiger to bed and . . .

Libby looked at the boy playing with a little glass domed paperweight, enclosing a group of children building a snowman. When it was turned upside down the scene became a blizzard. He was fascinated. Every time the white particles settled down he flipped it upside down once more and his merry peal of laughter made her laugh, too.

Everything was proceeding according to plan, until she decided that every family ought to have sugar cookies at Christmas. Hastily, she stirred up the ingredients, cleared the counter and sprinkled a heavy layer of flour across it. She turned the dough out in the center of the flour and reached for her rolling pin.

Tiger wandered to the window and began to jump up and down, yelling in excitement. "Will, Will." Before Libby realized what was happening, Tiger opened the window. A sudden gust of wind swooped through the opening and lifted the flour from the counter. Before Libby's eyes, the room began to look like Tiger's toy.

Will opened the door and looked around in amazement at the flour-covered room. He began to laugh as a small white whirlwind with legs plowed into him .

"Snow, Will, snow."

Libby looked around the room in dismay, heard Will's innocent, whistled edition of "Winter Wonderland," and joined in the laughter.

She started toward Will and Tiger, gasping now to catch her breath. Her bare feet hit the flour-slicked linoleum and slid her straight into them, sending both Will and Tiger sprawling. When she sat up, Will was powdered white. Libby started to laugh. Will joined in and they held each other while tears of laughter rolled down their snowman faces. Libby caught her sides as a stitch threatened her breath.

"Oh, no. I smell something burning." Libby

scrambled to her feet and dashed to the stove. The chicken pie was salvageable, but the homemade rolls were a total loss.

"Sorry, Will," she said with a sheepish look. "Looks like I've really made a mess of everything. And you had the apartment so nice and clean. I'm sorry."

"I'm not," he said and walked over to where she was looking at the burned rolls. "I've never been happier to see a mess in my life, if it brings the two people I care most about back home. He put his arms around her and kissed her, oblivious to the film of white that covered them both. If Tiger said anything, Libby didn't hear it. A faint ringing of bells vibrated across her mind, and she realized with amazement that it was just like in Angel's book. They were touching each other and it was good. She tightened her arms around Will's neck, and opened her lips, welcoming his tongue deep inside.

"Whee, lady. You ought to move out more often." Will pulled away and looked down at her with pride and something more in his eyes. The bells continued to ring and Libby realized with amusement that the sound she heard came from the church around the corner, not the power of Will's kiss. Well, she thought, so much for books, who needs them tonight? We've got the real thing.

Later, Tiger dusted, Will vacuumed and she tried to bring some order to dinner. So what if the sugar cookies became cakes. Will and Tiger didn't care. It was the spirit of the thing that counted, they both agreed.

Will put Tiger to bed and though it was early,

Libby took a shower, found her old granny gown, and crawled into bed. Will was right behind her and for once, he didn't have a technical magazine in his hand.

He turned to her, not with feathery teasing fingertips like she'd read, but his hands were gentle and loving. The granny gown didn't stay on long and after a quick exploration of her body he rolled eagerly over her and she willingly gave herself to him. If the loving wasn't earth-shattering, it was enough, she thought happily. Who knows, with more evenings like tonight to practice, they might get it right in another six years. When Will kissed her lovingly and pulled her close, she told herself that some women didn't even have that. The vague sense of discomfort that kept her tense for such a long time after Will slept gradually subsided and she, too, went to sleep.

When Stephen Colter crept into her dream and held out his arms, the physical reaction he invoked was like a powerful magnet and even in her dream she moaned and tried to turn away. It's only a dream, she told herself, but her body refused to accept her restraint and when he threw her down on the beach at the edge of a pounding surf, she felt herself respond in an overwhelming tide of passion that rocked her body with its climax. She felt the trembling subside as Will's arms clasped her in a comforting gesture of contentment.

"Nightmares, Libby? Don't worry, I'm here." He kissed her tenderly and touched his finger gently to her cheek.

"I won't, Will," she said and clung to him, not

from fear, but desperation, not from need, but desire, and—guilt. Eventually, she slept.

When she woke, the bed was empty and Will was already dressed and preparing breakfast. "Bad night, Libby?" Will was buttering toast.

"No, just excited, I guess. You know how I am about Christmas," she answered, trying not to remember the source of her discomfort. "I thought, if you have to work, I might take Tiger and let him spend the morning with Miss Lois. The bank closes at noon, I'll pick him up, and we can leave for your folks."

"I've a better idea. Do you think the bank would fall down if you didn't show up today?"

"No I guess not." She thought about Stephen's trip to Connecticut. Mrs. Hadley wouldn't approve but, after all, Libby was part of top management now and theoretically Mrs. Hadley's boss. Why not? "I'll just call in and tell them that Mrs. Spencer won't be in this morning. She's having an affair with Santa."

"An affair?" Will repeated curiously.

SIX

An hour later Tiger, Will and Libby Spencer were packed and heading down the interstate toward home and memories of the past.

Libby adjusted the sunglasses on her face and thought longingly about the pristine, snow-covered Christmas cards she had lined up across the mantelpiece. Georgia Christmas weather was better than Florida Christmas weather, but not much. Somehow, if you couldn't have snow, you ought to at least not have bright sunshine and sixty degrees. By late afternoon, they'd removed their sweaters and opened the windows.

"We're almost there, Tiger." Will interrupted the sixteenth chorus of "Jingle Bells," and Libby was more than glad to spot the turn off to the street where she'd grown up.

"Do you suppose your folks have informed half of Summerfield that we are coming?"

"You know Mama," he said with a shrug. "I'll

bet before we get the car unloaded someone will come by to see if we really brought a Vietnamese child home.''

"You told your mom?'' Libby felt awful. She hadn't even thought about asking permission. That realization told her how preoccupied she'd been for the last few days.

"Sure. I told her to get out the Santa suit and have Dad start practicing his ho-ho's.''

Will was wrong about how soon someone would come by. Someone was already there, standing on the front porch.

"Libby,'' Linda Sue Steeley called out gaily. "When I heard you were coming home for Christmas, I just simply had to come by. Mother sent one of her red velvet cakes for Mrs. Spencer. You know she's famous for them.''

Libby looked at Will, wondering if he remembered the last time Linda Sue Steeley had shared a cake with him. It had been on his sixteenth birthday. Libby had caught sight of them in the local ice cream parlor, sharing a hot fudge cake.

Libby had been crushed. Will had never noticed another girl before. That summer he'd suddenly discovered that Linda Sue was a new phenomenon to be studied. Linda Sue was a young woman and Will was growing up.

Libby had hurried home, borrowed her mother's eyeshadow and bright red lipstick, and tried to emulate Linda. But it hadn't been Will that discovered her propped seductively against the gate, it had been Pop. He'd scrubbed her face and sent her to her room. Later, he'd showed up with a cup of cocoa and explained that Will was growing up and that if she really wanted him she'd learn that being herself was more important than trying to be someone else.

The appearance of a new comet on the same night as Linda Sue's Sweet-Sixteen party had brought a dramatic end to Linda Sue and Will's tenuous relationship. Will had forgotten about Linda's birthday party. It had been twelve-year-old Libby who lay beneath the stars and watched the heavens with Will. After that, it was Libby who became Will's companion once more.

"And this is the little boy," Linda Sue was saying. "My, small isn't he?" She moved to Will's side and patted Tiger's head. She couldn't have gotten any closer to Will if she'd leaned on him.

Libby wanted to hit her. "So would you be, if you had your arm cut off and had to live in the street. Excuse us please, Linda Sue." Libby took Tiger's hand and led him inside, surprised at the animosity she still felt. Libby knew that she'd been rude. Tough! Linda Sue was Will's friend, let him sooth the situation.

"Libby," Addie Spencer's smile and warm voice always made a lump in Libby's throat, and she automatically leaned into arms that still welcomed her and comforted her. "I didn't hear you drive up. That Steeley girl found an excuse to come flying over here as soon as she heard Will was coming today. You'd think after all this time she'd get over her crush. He never looked at anybody else but you."

"And he didn't do much of that," Libby grumbled.

"What?" Mrs. Spencer unfolded her arms and leaned away. "What did you say, dear?"

"Oh, nothing. Just that he's been so busy designing an arm for Tiger here that he's not even looked at me lately. Until now, anyway. Linda Sue is plain out of luck. The line forms at the rear."

Mrs. Spencer dropped down and smiled at the child who huddled close to Libby, unsure of what was happening but trusting as he waited. "My goodness. He is a tiny one, isn't he? Can he talk?"

"He's learned a few words. Whatever you do, don't mention J-I-N-G-L-E B-E-L-L-S. He doesn't know what he's saying, but between the hospital and Will, he's learned every word and a few innovative new stanzas in addition. I've heard it for the last two hours."

"You sound tired, Libby, not like yourself. Why don't you let him come with me while you go unpack and take a nap?" She reached in her apron pocket and pulled out a molded gingerbread boy and held it out to Tiger.

"Cookie?" He took her hand and grinned happily. He knew full well what a cookie was, and if Libby said it was all right, that was all he needed. He went with Mrs. Spencer willingly. Libby heard Will come in the front door and follow her up the steps.

"Whee, I didn't realize we had so many Christmas presents. I don't remember these." He was holding the purchases from Rich's she had slipped in the car when he was packing.

"That's just a little surprise of mine. Bring them in our bedroom and put them in the closet, and don't peek."

Will followed her directions, then turned and swept her up in his arms. "You mean you expect me to leave these packages right here, unwrapped and undisturbed after I've been told not to look. Libby, surely you jest. I never could resist looking at something hidden." He leaned down and what started as a kiss ended with little nips on her ear.

Will Spencer nibbling on her ear. She couldn't believe it. Libby felt his hand slip under her sweater and slide suggestively toward her breast, she thought surely she was dreaming with her eyes wide open.

"Will," Libby said in a shocked voice and attempted to twist away, looking anxiously past him into the hallway. "Suppose someone sees you?"

"Suppose they do?" He held her, moving his lips around under her chin to the vee between her breast. "It's all right, Libby. We're married. I don't have to sit and hold onto my windowsill to keep from jumping through it and ripping off that skimpy little bikini you almost wore while you paraded all over the backyard that last summer before you graduated from high school."

"I didn't think you even noticed. Why didn't you say something? I thought I was ugly or that you weren't interested, or . . ." What she thought was getting lost in the rising fan of heat that spread itself up her body.

"Oh, I always noticed. Did you know that if I adjusted my telescope just right I could actually see . . ." His hand left her breast, unsnapped her jeans and worked itself down to the soft, downy hair between her legs. "I could actually see *this*, along the edge of that little string you had tied around your body?"

"No," she whispered raggedly, forgetting completely where they were and giving in to the delicious sensations his fingers were creating. ''But I knew that if I climbed up in the apple tree at the house and adjusted Pop's binoculars just right, I could see in your bathroom. I was the only girl in the eighth grade who knew firsthand what the best-looking guy in high school really looked like.''

''Libby!'' Will's gasp and sudden stiffness in his back abruptly ended his confessions. The red flush across Will's face might have become even worse if they hadn't heard the dual steps of Mrs. Spencer and Tiger at the foot of the stairs.

''If you're not going to take a nap and want to get one of these cookies before Tiger eats them all, you'd better come to the kitchen,'' she called up the steps. ''Leave that stuff in the car until Dad gets home.''

''Great,'' Will said, frustration coloring his voice. ''Cookies. Leave it to mothers, they always seem to sense the best possible time to interrupt,'' and turned to follow his mother's suggestion, jutting his chin forward as he made an exaggerated motion to clear his throat. ''I even feel like I'm sixteen. I wish I'd known when I was sixteen what I know now.''

''Will?'' Libby couldn't resist reaching out and cupping his obvious erection. ''We could always pretend. Of course, I can't be sure, but I suspect that in this case, experience is definitely better.''

''Tiger and I have made some nice hot cocoa.''

''Great! Now she's serving cocoa. Look at me. I even look sixteen. I've got a hard-on and have to face my mother,'' he growled and started out the door. "Just so you know, Mrs. Spencer, I intend to make you pay for this later."

"Oh, Will," Libby couldn't resist calling down to him as he loped down the stairs, "better wash your hands. Goodness knows where they've been."

She unpacked and put away their clothes, humming merrily as she worked. She'd thought that loving Will would stop being awkward once they were married. But it hadn't.

It had seemed wrong, improper somehow. Even though Mr. and Mrs. Spencer were downstairs in the other part of the house, she always felt they could hear the springs creak. The first weekend they'd come home after they'd moved in together, her suitcase had gone in one room and Will's in the other. Later, when he'd come to her bed, she'd made Will run the water in the bathroom to mask any sound they made. They'd both been so uncomfortable that the tub hadn't even filled by the time they'd turned it off and Will had retreated to his own bed.

That seemed so long ago, Libby thought, smiling. But today, if Mrs. Spencer hadn't interrupted when she did, this was one time when Libby might have locked the door and made love to Will right there. Of course, she knew that wouldn't really have happened, but she thought about it and that was definitely something new.

When Libby entered the familiar old kitchen, she found Will, Tiger, and Mrs. Spencer gathered around the same old scarred maple table where she'd had cookies and milk when she'd been Tiger's age. "I'm thinking you made the wrong drink. This is almost lemonade weather."

"Now, Libby," Mrs. Spencer laughed. "Christmas is a state of mind. And my mind says hot chocolate, gingerbread, and popcorn."

"Well, since that's as close as we're going to come to a white Christmas, we'd better get the popcorn popper going." Will had a gingerbread man in one hand and a huge slice of red velvet cake on a saucer before him.

Tiger's face was already smeared red. His cake was gone from the plate. Libby reached for a napkin and began to wipe creamy icing from his face.

"Let him go, Libby. It's been a long time since I had a little boy around here. Let me see to him. If you don't want to have a nap, why don't you two take a walk around the neighborhood, save everybody from dropping in?"

"A nap would have been nice," Libby said straight-faced, as she looked square at Will, "but I don't think I can calm my nerves enough to sleep. Your son just gets so excited, about Christmas, I mean. I told him that this is the time of year when, if you get too nosy, you find out things you don't want to know."

Will pretended not to know what she was talking about. He opened the door and followed Libby into the sandy yard.

"Did you like her, Will?"

"Like who?"

"Linda Sue Steeley."

"Of course not."

"But I saw you at the ice cream parlor."

"Why in the world would you think that? I never

would have paid any attention except that I heard the boys say she would let a guy . . . I mean . . .''

"Did she?"

"I don't know. I never got the nerve to try."

They were walking down Minerva Lane, under a canopy of bare-limbed trees that looked as if something had taken great bites from the branches. Progress. Once the trees completely shaded the street with great green interlacing arms. The power company had chipped away on one side uncovering the precious lines so that nothing would interrupt watching the TV or cooking in the all-new microwave ovens. Now, the trees looked wounded.

They turned the corner and walked up the back street, up Libby's street that ran directly behind Will's.

"Oh look, Will, look. They've painted the shutters on my house orange. They've ruined my house! It looks like Halloween." She wanted to cry at the changed look of her house. She would always think of it as home, even though someone else lived there now.

"And they've cut down those rose vines that grew over the porch. I loved the smell of those roses when I would sit at my window in the dark after everyone was asleep.

"Things change, Libby," Will said seriously. "It looks nice, you'll have to admit. It's just different now."

"I don't want things to change, Will. Do you ever want to go back, do things over?"

"Well," he reached out and took her hand in his. "I think I might like to go back and check out my telescope view in person, instead of long distance. Providing, of course, you'd like to do the same.''

"Will Spencer, you've got a one-track mind," Libby said in her best schoolmarm voice. "And I absolutely love it."

"I hope so, Libby," he said in a strange, sad tone. "I hope so."

By the time they had made the circle and spoken to everyone along the way, it was beginning to turn cooler and darker. Christmas tree lights blinked in every window along with candles and wreaths, and on one roof a Santa and sleigh flew off toward a fat rising moon.

"It's good to be home, Libby, to hold your hand and just talk. We never do this anymore, do we? And I miss it. I think I've missed you Kathryn Elizabeth McHanie Spencer."

When Will kissed her then, she didn't care if Linda Sue Steeley and half of Summerfield were watching. She stood on tiptoes and kissed him back.

Addie Spencer's pot of oyster stew was a new experience for Tiger. But once he saw Will crumble "cookies" into his bowl, he was sold, and the pot was quickly emptied. By the time Ed Spencer brought out one of Addie's fruitcakes, the size of a hoop of cheese, and prepared the coffee pot for perking, Tiger was long gone.

"Dad, I just don't have any room left now," Will said regretfully. "I think I'll take a raincheck till later, tomorrow maybe." He pushed back his chair and went looking for Tiger who was sitting beside the Christmas tree, eyeing the packages underneath with excitement.

"Ha, when he gets done with turkey and dressing and homemade rolls, he'll be too full for ambroisia and cake then, too. Never could put any meat on those bones no matter how much I fed him."

"Hey, Mom," Will called from the living room. "Where's the special 'open me early' for Tiger?"

"Oh, no, you don't, Will." Libby scrambled to her feet, declined Addie's offer of desert with a shake of her head, and followed Will. "No opening of anything until after bath and pajamas."

While Will was getting Tiger ready for bed, Libby helped Addie Spencer clear away the supper remains.

"There's a party at Mayor Dayley's house tonight if you two would like to go," Ed Spencer said as he put the fruitcake away.

"Now, Ed, you know Will and parties," Libby said. "I can never get him to go anywhere."

"Never did like parties," Addie chuckled. "Do you remember the last birthday party he had?"

"I sure do." Libby smiled. "He never showed up. Found a turtle nest when the eggs were hatching and missed the whole thing."

They could hear Tiger's screams of laughter and Will's answering animal growls between splashes of water.

"I'll declare, Libby, I can't remember when Will has been so involved with something or somebody."

"I know, Addie. Tiger has made a new man of Will. He's certainly done something in two weeks that I haven't been able to do in six years." She nibbled on a hangnail, then hurried to cover up the jealousy she was sure Addie heard in her voice. "He's become so attached to the child that I'm afraid he's going to miss him when he goes back to his family in his own country. If Tiger didn't have a family, I think Will would keep him.''

"You know, the first time I saw you together you were about six and he was ten. So far as I know, there's never been anybody else for either one of you. I know that you two love each other. What's wrong?'' Addie asked casually as she wiped the counter.

"I don't know. I mean, I thought that things would be different. But Will is always busy. The time just hasn't been right.''

"But don't you want children? I can see how Will feels about them. And that's something you *can* do.''

"Yes,'' Libby admitted softly. "But we've never really talked about it. I always wanted children, at least two, but when? I always thought children came with the license.''

"Funny,'' Addie mused, "I always thought they came with the love. In my day, we didn't do so much planning, I guess.''

Came with the love. The words stayed in Libby's thoughts while she watched Will come up the hall with Tiger slung over his hip. Little beads of water dripped down Tiger's face. Will's shirt was almost as wet. It was hard to tell who had had the bath. They sat down on the floor by the tree and began examining the packages.

"Which one, Libby? Tiger is impatient, can't stand the suspense.''

Ed Spencer chuckled as he tapped the dead ashes from his pipe and repacked it with tobacco. "Seems to me like it's the big boy who's impatient, the little one is more interested in the Christmas tree lights.''

It was true, Tiger sat hypnotized by the blinking lights as well as the brightly colored packages. It was Will who fidgeted.

"All right," Addie laughed, dropping with a sigh to her easy chair opposite Ed. "You never could wait, could you? It's the small square one wrapped in the Santa Claus paper."

The tree trembled as Will shimmied under the bottom limbs to retrieve the proper package. He touched Tiger on the shoulder, swung him around and into his lap.

"Look, Tiger, for you." Somehow, with pointing and a large amount of help, Will conveyed the message that the gift was for Tiger and could be opened now.

"It's *The Night Before Christmas*," Addie explained as Tiger turned the pages, with eyes full of stars. "I thought he might be able to understand what is to happen, from the pictures. I mean Santa Claus does come on Christmas Eve, doesn't he? Or is that too old-fashioned?"

"You better believe it," Will said positively. "Santa Claus, that's one old-fashioned custom I don't ever plan to change."

As Tiger turned the pages, Will pulled a pillow from the couch, stretched out on the floor and took the book and began to read.

There was a warm silence about the room as they all listened. The rich smell of mincemeat pies cooking in the oven, the pine odor of the tree were all the familiar Christmas smells, and Libby settled down in peaceful contentment. She wished Pop was here to share this. He'd be right down there with Will and Tiger, just as he'd done with her. The only difference was that she was here, too, as Tiger's temporary mother, a part of the family scene, and her own mother never was.

Mr. Spencer was theoretically reading his newspaper, though his eyes followed Will and Tiger more than his newsprint. Addie was simply watching her family, her eyes filled with love. Libby watched Will as he pointed to the pictures and patiently pronounced the words. Tiger's mind was quick and it was amazing the progress he was making with English.

Will would miss Tiger, and perhaps she would, too. The analytical side of her mind knew that she and Will hadn't touched their real problems. They hadn't really talked. By some unspoken agreement they had avoided the real issues. He hadn't mentioned the roses, or her leaving. Everything had been postponed until after Christmas, or a better way to put it, after Tiger. When she was with Will, like he was now, this was all there was. Everything else faded away and she knew their life was just what she'd dreamed it would be.

Then why did Stephen Colter haunt her? Even now, when she least expected it, he intruded in her thoughts and made her feel guilty that she'd allowed him there. He was smart and efficient, and he listened to her. When she was around him, she felt smart and efficient and important, too. But what did she really know about him? And why should she be interested in knowing anything at all? It was only that her heart skipped when he touched her and the day came suddenly alive and she knew that was wrong. Why didn't she react to Will like that?

She looked at Addie Spencer. Did she ever feel her body tremble hungrily for something? Did she secretly touch herself and fantasize? Libby shook her head. In spite of the trend toward a woman reaching out for what she wanted, it bothered her that she, as a married woman, should fantasize. It was simply the overselling of sex everywhere she looked that made her feel such things. She knew she was lucky. Will loved her. That should be enough. It was her own foolish mind that reached out for something else.

"Well," Addie finally stood up. "I think it's time all us old folks went to bed." She touched a dozing Ed on the arm and put her finger to her lips, "Shhhhhhh."

Tiger and Will were both asleep. Libby came to her feet, lifted Tiger in her arms, and carried him to the small bedroom across from Addie and Ed. She wondered what had happened to his brown paper sack where he carried all his treasures. Maybe he didn't need it anymore.

"We'll listen out for him, Libby. Don't you and and Will worry. And," Addie whispered wickedly, "you don't really need to run the water anymore. Just between you and me, sometimes a woman has to help things along a bit, if she's married to a man who doesn't live in the real world."

Libby grinned sheepishly and whispered good night. She left the night-light burning, just as Pop had for her when she was a child, and gently closed the door. There was something good about this house, full of love and commitment between two people who believed children came with the love. In the living room, she sat back down and watched Will as he slept.

He was lying back against the cushions, all angled and helpless looking. She remembered seeing him like that before. Funny how it all went back to the beginning. Maybe it was just because they were home where the beginning started as her own childhood fantasy of "when I grow up and marry Will." It seemed so long ago, like a dream that belonged to someone else.

Will made a sound and suddenly she was back in Addie's living room. Libby looked down at him only to find him studying her with a strangely analytical expression.

"What're you thinking, Libby? You look so sad."

"Just thinking about Christmas, I guess, and Pop, and wondering where the time has gone."

"You sound like my dad. But you don't look a bit like him. Why don't you come down here with me and let me check out my haircut job, see if you're ready for another trim?"

"Aren't you going to put on the Santa suit and do the ho-ho bit for Tiger?"

"No, I thought about it, but he mightn't understand and, well, maybe I'll save it for our children, if we decide to have them. I think I'll wait. Maybe by then I'll fill the suit out a little better. Libby?"

Libby couldn't resist the need in Will's eyes and she slid down to the floor, welcoming the intimacy of closeness that folded about her. Maybe this time . . .

"I know this has been hard on you, Libby, my being so involved at the lab and the hospital. Then, bringing Tiger home without consulting you. At the time I just didn't stop to think. It's all been a surprise to me, too." His arm had curled around her shoulders and under her neck. She could feel the warmth of his breath against her face. She understood that he was surprised at his own actions and she answered the tightening of his grip by encircling his body with her arm and resting her head on his chest.

"You know," he went on, "it's funny, I haven't thought much about you and me. We just were. The challenge was knowing that I could make ideas come to life, do things they said couldn't be done. Once I have even a glimmer of new knowledge, I close everything out until I understand it. I don't mean to, it just happens."

"I know," Libby said softly. "You have tunnel vision and I'm not the vision at the end of the tunnel. I'm always the everything that gets closed out. I never used to mind, but I do now, Will. I have to tell you that something just isn't right between us. I know it's probably my fault."

"No. Don't blame yourself. It isn't your fault," Will whispered, "and just as soon as I get Tiger's arm squared away, I'm going to concentrate on us, I promise. I'll figure it out."

Libby surrendered to his promises and his kisses, giving herself to the contentment of present need and past remembering. She pushed aside the promises

Will had made before. It was going to be different this time, she'd make it be.

The wild surge of need in her body seemed joined in the kaleidoscope of rainbow color and like the tumultuous up and down of riding a roller coaster. It rose and fell in a current of hot response. When Will stood up and took her by the hand, she went willingly up the stairs.

Inside the room, he began to undress her. She was so ready that for once she didn't even think about where they were. Will laid her back on the bed and began to remove his own clothes, standing hesitantly over her until she held out her arms.

Libby loved making love. She always had. The feeling, the closeness, it was more than she'd ever suspected and this time, she reached for that elusive moment, knowing that it was close, urging, seeking the release of the tidal wave that was threatening to burst though the clenched muscles of her woman parts. So close, So close. Then, Will shuddered and fell against her in a subsiding moan.

Libby caught her lip between her teeth in despair. She knew that, as wonderful as it had been, there had to be more. She'd been so close and now it was gone. But for tonight, she told herself patiently—it was Christmas, a time of love—this was enough.

The chime of the antique kitchen wall clock broke the silence and Libby raised up on one elbow looked down at Will and managed the expected smile, the smile that always said thank you. "If Santa isn't pooped, I have another job for him. We have to put Tiger's presents from Santa Claus under the tree."

"The spirit's willing, babe, but the body needs

help this time before it can get up and go again. Come to think of it, with treats like you under the Christmas tree, I have my doubts that Santa will ever get his rounds made."

Will did love her. Libby could see it in his eyes as he looked up at her. She knew she had something few women had. If only . . . only what? She simply didn't know.

Chill bumps replaced passion and reluctantly they redressed and took the packages out of the closet. When Will saw the train set Libby had bought, he was immediately wild to try it out. Lovingly, he set it up beside the hotwheels and other games he'd bought. While he was admiring the train, Libby hid the toy she'd bought for Will behind a chair. When they'd finished, Libby stood back, surveying the tree and gifts, Will's arm slung over her shoulders in total rare contentment.

"Merry Christmas, babe." He swung around, dropping both arms under her buttocks, and rested his chin against her forehead. "You know, if I knew how to dance, I would."

"I'll teach you," Libby whispered, eagerly. "Maybe we could go out someplace . . . special New Year's Eve, dress up and go dancing?"

"Well—maybe—we'll see, Lib. You know how I am about parties. Oh . . . I couldn't wrap your Christmas present, but I hope you'll like what this represents." He reached into his pocket and handed her a large brass key.

"I don't understand, what is it?"

"It's a house key, babe. I thought . . . if you

want, after the first of the year, we might look around . . . I mean . . .''

A house key? Libby was astonished. For years a home of their own had been part of her plan. But Will had put it off. He hadn't seemed to be interested. What they had was fine for him. Now a house? Wasn't this what she'd always wanted? Why was it such a surprise? She didn't know what to say.

Will stopped swaying to the imaginary music and said, ''Don't you like it? I thought . . .''

''Of course, I do,'' Libby said positively, falling back into the circle of his arms. ''Of course, I do. I'm just so surprised. Thank you, Will.'' She stood on tiptoes and kissed him, covering the confusion she was feeling, then added, ''If we don't dance up to bed, we won't be able to get up and I know how much you want to play with that electric train.''

''Not as much as I want to play with you, Libby.''

After Will released her and went to the wall to snap out the lights, Libby stood in a kind of wooden shock for a moment, before she realized that he was already halfway up the steps. Quickly, she slipped the crazy monkey with the clapping symbols from behind the chair and placed it in the circle made by the train, making sure the tag with *To Will from Santa* in big red letters was still attached.

''Where are you, babe?''

''Here, Will,'' she whispered unsteadily. ''I'm here, behind you, right where I've always been.''

SEVEN

"Merry Christmas, Merry Christmas. Ho! Ho! Ho! Will."

A whirlwind of movement hit the bed. Libby felt the frame shake and wooden slats groan.

"Will, Will. See, see. Ho! Ho!" Tiger was a record, repeating his newly-acquired Christmas jargon over and over, as he tugged futilely on Will's hand.

"Libby, I think Tiger has just learned about Santa Claus." Will threw back the covers, swept Tiger up in the air, and whirled him around, depositing him in the warm spot where his body had been.

"You wait right there and let me dress," he directed, pulling his jeans over his briefs and slipping his bare feet into sneakers.

Libby yawned and looked at her watch. "Well, he did better than we used to. It's eight o'clock."

Will had added a light pullover sweater and was ready. He was almost as anxious as Tiger. He lifted

Tiger and headed for the door, stopped suddenly, and turned back to Libby. "Nope, Tiger, we have to wait on Libby. She's part of this, too. Have to learn patience."

"Patience?" Always before it had been up to Libby to catch up. Now, Will was waiting for her. She hurried.

But patience turned out to be in short supply and before Libby had combed her hair, Will and Tiger had dragged her, protesting, to the Christmas tree. Will looked at the monkey, then back to Libby, a big grin plastered from ear to ear.

Libby gave him a grin in return. It was hard to tell which was the child. Mr. Spencer quickly located an old engineer's gray striped cap and commanded the train controls. Will wound up the key on the toy monkey and the noise began. Between Tiger's squeals, the whistle of the train, and Mr. Spencer's directing of the action, Libby and Mrs. Spencer quickly sought refuge in the kitchen.

"There's absolutely no point in making breakfast. They won't eat half of it and before we are done cleaning up behind them they'll be starving for turkey. Just give them coffee and doughnuts, and the boy can have milk."

Addie quickly perked the pot of coffee Ed had prepared but never used the night before. "As for me," she confided, "I'm going to have a big chunk of fruit cake with my coffee."

Libby agreed and began to help lay out the food. "Did Will tell you what he's getting me for Christmas?"

"No, but that's no surprise. Even as a boy he

never was much for talking about doing a thing. He either did, or didn't. His daddy and I never knew what to expect."

"This." Libby held up the large brass key.

"Um. Looks like a trunk key to me. You taking a trip?"

"No, it's a house key. A key to the new house we're going to look for at the first of the year."

"You don't sound so happy about it. Doubts?"

"No. I mean, yes. I mean I don't know. It's that I've waited so long for Will to talk about our future. And he never has. I don't know what's wrong with me. I'm suddenly not sure."

"Nothing so strange about that. A dream's a comfortable thing to carry around. It's somewhere off in the future, makes no demands and you don't have anything to do with it. But when it becomes a reality, that's something else. You're staring it straight in the face. It's now and you're forced to assume responsibility for its outcome."

"Libby, Mom, come on in and let's open the gifts." Will called into the kitchen.

Addie carried two mugs of coffee and Libby followed with the platter of doughnuts and a mug of milk for Tiger.

Will played Santa and passed out the presents under the tree and, miraculously enough, none of the coffee and milk was spilled.

The Spencers's gift for Libby was a creamy white velour robe. "You couldn't have made a more appropriate choice," she said sincerely. "My old quilted robe is battle scarred and ready for burial at sea."

Addie and Ed liked their matching blue sweaters.

And Will's eyes took on a particularly wicked gleam when he opened his matching white robe from his folks. But his expression was more puzzled over the book Libby had bought. The salesman had assured her that any man would thoroughly enjoy the humorous how-to-please-a-woman approach the author had taken in writing the book. It hadn't been quite the same as Angel Harper's sex secrets, and Libby hoped the outcome wouldn't be as disastrous.

When Tiger opened his gift of cap pistols and caps, Libby and Addie Spencer escaped once more.

"Don't know why Will didn't latch onto a little girl. It sure would have been quieter," Addie commented as she bustled about the kitchen.

"Yes," Libby agreed, thinking about the baby doll she'd bought so impulsively and hidden away in the hall closet at home.

By the time Libby and Mrs. Spencer placed the turkey and dressing on the already overflowing table, Will had taught Tiger how to lean into the curves and he was a onehanded super jock in his new hotwheels go-car.

Libby was finally forced to take away the monkey, unplug the train, and banish the cap pistol before she could pry the men away from the toys.

After lunch, they cleared away the aftermath and watched the fireplace burn up the bright wrappings of a Christmas day rapidly coming to a close. All things considered, Libby decided the day had gone very well. Tiger was tired and lay quietly on the rug, his toys surrounding him. Ed, wearing his new bright blue sweater, lazed by the fireplace, smoking his pipe. And Will lay with his head in a copy of some technical manual that had been a gift from Pat. Libby almost hated to remind Will that they ought to be heading home.

They packed up enough food to eat all week, the rest of Addie's fruit cake, and the gifts. The trip back was quiet. They were all tired. Tiger was soon sleeping on the backseat.

"Does Tiger know that he has to report to the hospital in the morning?" Libby asked as they reached the outskirts of town. "I mean, isn't it wrong to give him all this, then have to separate him from it right away?"

"Who's separating him? Everyone of these things goes to the hospital with him. He'll have a few days before the surgery and the toys will make it easier. The more content he is there, the better his recovery will be. And, yes, he knows about the surgery and he's going to face it like an adult."

"No dreams for him," Libby murmured. "Just look reality straight in the face."

Later, unpacked in bed, she wondered, *Why is everybody so wise, except me?* Libby squirmed. No shifting frame, no groaning slats, this bed was sturdy enough to take a pounding. It just rarely had to. Poor Santa, he'd worn himself out last night. He had fallen sound asleep as soon as his head hit the pillow.

Libby flipped back the extra weight of the blanket. It was just too warm. Another mild Christmas seemed destined to mock her childhood dreams of snow and sleighs and picture-book scenes.

Snow, Connecticut, Stephen. She didn't want to think about Stephen. Libby tried to concentrate on the happiness of the day. The warmth of Will's outpouring of love and newly unleashed romantic approach was still close to her and she tried desperately to keep Stephen's face from intruding.

As hard as she tried to get rid of his image, there he was: golden ski suit outlined against a snow-covered hill; rushing down a mountain, head thrown back challenging the world with a wink and the back of his hand. Suddenly, she closed her eyes and she was there, too, back in the snow-covered lodge, arms entwined with Stephen's as they danced in the mellow darkness. She felt her body suddenly come alive, nerve endings tingling as she felt the flush of desire that washed across her body. She tried not to move, afraid that Will would wake, then afraid he wouldn't. She couldn't be still any longer.

Finally, she left the bed and wandered unsteadily through the darkness toward the kitchen. The Christmas tree stood dark and bare looking without its gifts. It seemed to be hiding in the shadowy living room. From the kitchen window she could see out into the empty street below. The watery circle of light that washed away from the street light into the blackness seemed pale and uncertain. Why was she so strung out? The lightness and teasing tenderness that Will had showered over her, the day, everything had been just as she had imagined it would be. She couldn't have asked for more.

Libby tried to understand her disappointment. Perhaps she was experiencing the normal holiday letdown. She could see the brass key Will had given her. It lay on the kitchen counter like the holy grail, both fascinating and repelling. She wanted to fling it in the garbage; to say to Will, Not yet, I'm not ready. Still, she knew that she couldn't hide behind the thought that Will had let her down by not providing one of the major ingredients of her well-made plans. He'd done his part. Now, she must do hers and be excited about their future.

Unwanted tears welled up in her eyes and she reached for a tissue in the pocket of her old housecoat pocket. The pocket was empty—all the tissues were gone. The card that had come with the flowers wasn't there either. She distinctly remembered slipping it inside her housecoat pocket. Where had she dropped it? It seemed so long ago, that night when Tiger had first come into their lives and Stephen had sent the pink roses. The card was gone, but the words still haunted her.

"Yesterday, today, and—"

"Why don't you check the housing want ads in today's paper, Libby. We ought to start getting an idea about what's available and what it will cost." Will was finishing his bowl of cornflakes and milk, and encouraging Tiger to do the same while Libby began to clear the dishes.

"Do you really think it will be possible for us to buy a house, Will? I mean, do we have enough money for that kind of purchase?"

"We'll manage. Once I get this new concept developed, we'll be able to buy a lot of things. It's too early to talk about it, but I'm sure it will work out. For now, it's just a matter of raising the money. I hate that part of research. If I could just find a little money here and there for parts."

"That's what I wanted to talk to you about, Will,

finding money here and there. I know you won't like it, but Dixie is having a party New Year's Eve. She wants to give it in your honor to raise money for your artificial arms' project. That's something I—she and I can do to help you. Isn't that a great idea?''

Will very carefully laid down his spoon, wiped his lips with his napkin, and looked straight at Libby.

Libby held her breath, knowing what was coming, yet hoping she was wrong. This was her first attempt to contribute to Will's work and she wanted him to be pleased.

''Dixie wants to do what?'' Will's anger cut through her pride like a sudden painful blanket of icy wind.

''She's planned a special New Year's Eve party in your honor, Will, to help raise money for your project. We . . .''

''Libby, in the six years we've been—together—have I ever attended one of Dixie's fancy parties?'' He had moved directly across from Libby, holding her with invisible barbs of energy, daring her to move or reply.

''No,'' she whispered, raggedly. She should have known he wouldn't cooperate, but she'd thought perhaps now things were better. She'd tried to warn Dixie that Will had his own ideas about parties and nothing would budge him, not even her.

''Good. Since you understand, you explain. I am not going anywhere on New Year's Eve. Raise money for my project? What makes you two think any of her scatterbrained, society misfits have any money, or plan to part with it if they do?''

''But, Will, what about *our* New Year's Eve? I

thought maybe we could . . . never mind," she whispered in customary defeat. "It doesn't matter what I want to do anyway. It never has."

Libby had intended to be strong, persuasive, convince Will that she had something to offer, that she could be a part of his life. Now, she was cowering in defeat. It was no use. Will just didn't care about having friends and outside interests. Nothing she could do would ever change that. He meant well, he just never quite had time for outsiders. She could have sat down with a stranger and explained, and the stranger would have listened and understood about her needing people.

Stephen would have listened, she told herself wistfully. He listened to her at the office. What was more important, he appreciated her ideas, about banking anyway. Libby heard the door slam. Both Tiger and Will were gone and Will hadn't even said goodbye. The Christmas spirit hadn't lasted very long.

Suddenly, Libby was angry and she was hurt. She had needs, too. What she needed was someone who understood—she needed Stephen, needed the reassurance of his confidence and caring. She couldn't wait to get downtown.

The downtown parking lot was almost empty this week between Christmas and New Year's, and Libby found a spot easily. She glanced in the mirror, noting the brightness of her large brown eyes heavily fringed with dark lashes. An urgency captured her and she quickly drew a comb through her hair, leaving it loose about her face, and went inside. She nodded crisply at the clerical staff manning the outer office, aware of the respectful deference she now enjoyed as Stephen's assistant. Everybody else knew of her importance, everybody except Will. She hadn't even told her own husband about her promotion.

"Good morning, Mrs. Hadley. Did you have a nice holiday?"

"Good morning, Mrs. Spencer. And, yes I did, thank you. Mr. Colter would like you to come to his office right away."

In spite of their close working relationship of the last week, Libby knew that Mrs. Hadley resented Libby's being chosen to assist in the transition and she felt the glare of her disapproval all the way across the reception area.

"Libby." Stephen's voice told her how glad he was to see her. Blue eyes captured her with a burning intensity that spoke more deeply than words.

She felt a tremor as the floor seemed to shift slightly beneath her feet. She was back to liquid waterbeds again.

"Good morning, Mr. Colter," she managed to say, in what she hoped was her best assistant-to-the-vice-president voice. "You wanted me?"

"Yes, Mrs. Spencer, I do. I most certainly do and if I didn't know it before, this weekend without you has made it definitely clear.

Libby knew the question he was answering hadn't been voiced. She turned quickly away, making a big production of removing her coat and hanging it on the rack by the door.

She knew that she'd purposefully worn the burnt-orange knit dress because it hugged her body and gave her curves that nature hadn't intended. Nervously, she cleared her throat and turned back to see the amused expression flicker at the corner of Stephen's mouth.

"What's on the schedule for today, Mr. Colter?"

"What I have on my schedule and what I have on my mind are two different things. But, I can see from your body language, that it's business before pleasure, for now." He turned reluctantly to his desk, blue eyes raking her once more with a promise of later.

By lunchtime, they had narrowed down the lists of personnel to be transferred and defined their duties based on the central computer, and had worked out a time frame for the changes. Libby knew the original plans called for closing some of the branch banks and she'd worked hard on suggesting ways to keep them open while still complying with the policies set by the transition committee.

They worked well together, Libby decided. Stephen mentioned something and she immediately understood. He asked for, and more often than not, took her suggestions. Everything was exciting and stimulating.

"What did Santa leave under your tree, Libby?"

Libby felt her face flame as she remembered the lovemaking under the Christmas tree. "Uh, a brass key," she stammered, knowing the scent of Stephen's cologne made her body feel as if it were contracting into some tight knot of charged particles.

"Boy, that sounds like a real winner."

"It is," she defended. "A key to the new house we're going to buy."

"With a white picket fence, with a boy for him, and a girl for you? No," Stephen said, "that's not where I see you. You belong in the penthouse, with designer dresses, and flying to Europe today and Dallas tomorrow. We're a team, Libby. You know it and so do I.'' All morning he'd managed to touch her shoulder, reach across her with arms just brushing her breasts. She'd never been so aware of a man and she was glad that lunchtime was at hand. The confines of the office were closing in and she needed space and people and time.

It seemed only natural to accept Stephen's invitation to lunch. When they left together, she knew from the glances of the main-level personnel that she was the envy of all the women in the bank, and she felt a sense of exhilaration.

The circular bubble atop the seventy-story hotel was a favorite place to lunch in the downtown area. In the late December sunlight, it offered a panoramic view of the five-county metropolitan area.

"Doesn't feel much like Christmas," Stephen commented as the hostess showed them to a table.

"No," Libby agreed. "Not the weather, anyway. When I was a child, I always wished for the kind of Christmas that was on the Currier and Ives Christmas cards with snow and horse-drawn sleighs.''

"You would have loved Christmas in Connecticut. It was just what you ordered." There was a warmth in Stephen's manner and Libby felt the same electricity she'd tried so hard to ignore.

"With Barbara Stanwyck?" she questioned, hastily trying to break the mood that was rapidly becoming more than a business lunch. She knew it was probably the romantic in her that made her so susceptible to the forbidden. The grass was always greener and all those things.

"No, not Barbara Stanwyck, though the lady who was my hostess is a writer. But mysteries, not cookbooks."

"You remember that movie?" Libby was amazed. Will always laughed at her interest in old movies. But she loved all those oldies, particularly at Christmas, and she watched every one. *White Christmas*, *Miracle on 34th Street*, but *Christmas in Connecticut* had always been her favorite.

"Of course," Stephen supplied, "With Dennis Morgan and that marvelous old character actor that played her cook . . . Felix something or other."

By the time they reached desert, Libby was forced to admit that Stephen's knowledge of old movie trivia surpassed her own. "Goodness, Stephen," she remembered guiltily, "we've been gone well over an hour. What will Mrs. Hadley say?"

"Probably that we're sharing more than a two-cocktail lunch." His tone went suddenly serious and Libby felt her heart drop when his hand closed over her own. The moment she had been avoiding had come.

"But, Stephen . . ."

"I don't mind being cast as a villain or the other man, if I'm really guilty," he said seriously. "You know there's something between us, Libby. There has been from the beginning. In my mind, your husband is the other man. After all, I was first. I find I don't want to see our work here come to an end. I want you with me."

There was a long, emotional moment. Libby didn't

know what to say. Her throat was dry and she couldn't speak.

Then, as if from one of those old movies, a voice pierced the silence.

"Libby? It is you. I didn't see you when I came in."

Libby jerked her hand guiltily away and looked up into the puzzled eyes of Will's cronie, Pat Pilcher. "Oh, hello, Pat," Libby managed to say, knowing the red blush that swept across her face spoke her guilt louder than her stammering response. She took a deep breath and tried to ignore the sense of guilt she felt at the result of Pat's accusing glance. "This is Mr. Colter, my employer. Mr. Colter, Pat Pilcher, my husband, Will's . . . associate."

"Pat Pilcher and Will Spencer. My god, Libby, is your husband the Will Spencer who is working on the first artificial limb to be permanently attached to the human body?"

"Well, I suppose that's what he's doing. I didn't know that it was to be permanently attached." Libby became totally confused at Stephen's enthusiasm and before she realized what was happening, Stephen and Pat were animatedly discussing the new breakthrough that was making Will a celebrity in some investment magazine highlighting future geniuses.

When at last Pat insisted that he had to rejoin his own party, Libby found herself promising to introduce Stephen to Will before Stephen's assignment was complete.

"I can't believe Will Spencer is your husband," Stephen said repeatedly as they returned to the bank.

"He is doing some truly remarkable work in his field. Though his theories are yet to be proven, my financial advisors tell me he's a very good investment if he ever decided to market his ideas."

"I don't understand," Libby admitted. "If he's so well known, why does he need more money. I mean, I thought his projects were all in the red." Libby couldn't believe that she was asking Stephen about Will's work.

"True," Stephen confirmed. "He's known as an honest man, a humanitarian who donates his skills, his knowledge to help those who are not in a position to help themselves. So far, none of the manufacturers have been able to lure him away from the university. They've offered him the moon, but he keeps refusing."

"Why?"

"If he goes with the manufacturer, he loses control and his freedom to follow his own interests. By working through the county hospital, he is able to make his prototype available to anyone he chooses and everything, including the hospital bill, is free. Then, when the prototype is perfected, the university sells it and recoups its money."

"Tiger benefits," she said softly. "As do all my old friends in the retirement complex who couldn't afford the medical work they receive through the county hospital if they went anywhere else."

"The university and the hospital reap the benefits of his knowledge and his reputation," Stephen went on. "I think he's a fool, but I admire him. That's quite a man you're married to. The gossip is that he's being touted for a Nobel Prize."

Libby was totally shocked. Will a Nobel Prize-winner? It didn't seem possible. And he'd never mentioned it. The man who wanted to be her lover knew more about her husband than she did. Why hadn't he said something? Was this part of the talk they were to have after Tiger's operation?

The rest of the day was a jumble of mixed emotions. Libby couldn't shake off the guilt of being caught in an intimate lunch with Stephen. That it was Will's best friend made it all the more damaging. And she was forced to face the fact that had Pat not appeared, she might have done something even more foolish.

Her mood alternated between chagrin and anger. Will never told her about the articles in the magazines. Even Pat hadn't mentioned it. Of course, she had to admit that she never spent much time around Pat. Whenever he and Will got together, they talked about technical things, and she felt out of place and found something else to do. Generally, she cleaned the apartment, or cooked, or found a romance novel and a quiet place alone. The afternoon passed in a haze of confusion and suddenly everyone was gone.

When Stephen asked her to work late, she looked away from the ever-present question in his eyes, shaking her head in refusal. Everything was happening so fast. She was afraid to be alone with Stephen because her body was rapidly overpowering her mind and she sensed that this time there would be no turning back.

All the way home she asked herself why Will's touch and glance didn't set her body throbbing like Stephen's. For once, she understood Will's preoccupation with jogging. She wanted to walk or run or cry, to find some kind of physical release from the turmoil building inside of her.

She'd barely closed the apartment door behind her when the building custodian delivered a brightly-wrapped package that had come by messenger that afternoon, with instructions that she be given the present later. But the custodian was going to a party and didn't think it would matter if he came a little earlier.

Libby opened it with both anticipation and reluctance. The tiny ivory unicorn inside was set with brilliant red-jeweled eyes and a clamp that fastened it as a broach. Libby gasped at the luminous quality and superb detail in the workmanship. With trembling fingers, she opened the envelope and read the card: "May the New Year fill your life with fantasies come true."

Thank goodness the building custodian had come up early, or Will would have been home. Unless Stephen intended that Will should know. Maybe an answer was being forced on her. What had he meant when he'd said, I want you with me?

Libby heard the sound of Will's key in the lock, crumpled the wrappings and dropped them hastily into the fireplace. The unicorn went into her purse. She was hanging up her coat in the closet when Will came in the bedroom. The stern set of his lips was a continuation of his morning displeasure and she waited for him to mention Pat's having seen her at lunch.

"I hope you and little Miss Fix-It are proud of yourselves." He wrenched off his tie, unbuttoned his shirt and slung it toward the doorknob.

"What do you mean, Will?"

"Don't try to pretend innocence with me. Everything about this New Year's Eve celebration has been planned by you, dear wife, and your flaky friend. I suppose you don't know that Dixie went to the department head and explained her little fund-raising scheme?"

"She did?"

"Sure you know. You were in it right up to your wide-open little eyes." He stepped out of a loafer and slung it savagely toward the closet. "I'm not interested in politicking with those gold-plated phonies. I don't have time to waste like that. Certainly not on the same day Tiger is scheduled for surgery. If this is what you want, you go. I'll be at the hospital."

"Will, I don't know what you are talking about. If Dixie invited your boss to her party, she was only trying to make you see how important her help can be. She's trying to help. I realize how little I really know about your work, but I didn't know what she was doing." Suddenly, Libby was angry, too, really angry. And her words poured out in surging torrent.

"And I'll tell you something else, my shy, undercover genius, there seem to be a number of things *I* don't know. Why didn't you tell me about the magazine articles about you, or the companies trying to hire you? You're practically famous and I have to find out from an investment consultant who would like to market you."

"Libby," he said, coldly. "That's all publicity hype. You don't care about that anyway."

"Of course, I care. Didn't it occur to you that the

decisions you were making affected our future? As ignorant and unimportant as my opinion might be, don't you think I have the right to know? It's you who doesn't care. They're closing or merging Peachtree National Bank into Windsor Trust. Peachtree National is important to me, too. It will be no more. Do you know, or even care, what that means to those old people who depend on us? My work may not get me a Nobel Prize, but it's important, too."

An unexpected silence dropped over both of them. They'd never spoken to each other like this before. Only the sound of angry, uneven breathing filled the void.

"You're right, Lib," he agreed finally in an unexpectedly even tone. "I didn't know. But I didn't know because you didn't tell me."

"We don't tell each other anything, Will. When you're here, you really aren't. I'm just a convenience, nothing more."

"I guess we've both been going through our own separate crises. Maybe I'm as guilty as you." He ran his fingers through his hair in a resigned gesture and flopped down unexpectedly on the bed.

"All right," he said in resignation. "I'll go to the party. I'll make a speech and I'll even wear a tuxedo, as long as *I* don't have to rent it." He looked up with the old, little-boy grin and said with surprising humor, "Just don't get me any ruffles and promise me I won't have to dance. You know I can't dance, Libby."

"Do I, Will? I thought that's what we were doing Christmas Eve. I suppose it'll be next year before something like that happens between us again. That is, if you don't have something more important to do.''

Bitch, Libby thought, that's what she was. She pulled a turquoise velour shirt over her head and padded barefoot to the kitchen. She knew Will's comment about ruffles and dancing was meant to be an apology for railing out at her. Her own flippant response slipped out before she'd thought and she wished she could take back her words.

''Don't bother with dinner, Libby. I'd like to stay and talk about this, really talk about it, but I just can't. There's just not enough time left before Tiger's surgery and we're still checking out the arm. The computer calibration is just a hair out of sync and I can't seem to find the problem.''

Libby knew he was reluctant to leave, and for once he'd tried to explain the urgency of his leaving.

She was filling the teapot. She turned off the water and considered her words before answering. ''It's all right, Will. I'm beginning to understand something about your deadlines. Go on, Tiger's arm is important to both of us, maybe even more important to us than it is to him. I just need you, too, Will.'' *I need you to do something before I explode.*

Will turned back and brushed her lips softly at first, then more insistently for just a moment before making a little moan and drawing away. ''As soon as we get this behind us, we'll talk, Libby; about the bank, and you, and us.'' His voice was husky and he started to add something, shook his head, and caught her chin in long slim fingers. He kissed her once more and she wanted to hold on, some dread almost made her cry out her fear.

There had been a time when those words would have carried her for weeks. Not anymore. Everything had changed. She knew that their lives would never be the same again and she didn't know where they were going.

When Will was gone, Libby retrieved the ivory unicorn, a make-believe creature from the world of fantasy and romance—a fantasy like Stephen Colter. Whatever else she was, Libby was learning to be honest and she knew that Stephen was a fantasy come to life, a mystical creature that sprang from her dreams. Will was real and she must separate the two. Perhaps, she thought numbly as she closed her fingers around the tiny creature, the fantasy is what we create when love isn't enough.

EIGHT

The proposals and alternate recommendations for the bank merger were almost complete. Libby was glad. She was finding it harder and harder to concentrate on her work. Stephen's presence made her office seem small and closed in. Every breath she took was full of the musky smell of his cologne.

Earlier in the day, Dixie had told her that Stephen, as the representative for the powerful Windsor Trust Bank, had been invited to her New Year's Eve party and Libby's nerves were drawn even tauter. She didn't know how she would get through that night's celebration with both Will and Stephen in the same place.

"Mrs. Spencer?" Mrs. Hadley stood in the doorway. "There's a Miss Carter here to see you from the Volunteer Day Service."

"Volunteer Day Service? I don't know anything about volunteer service or Miss Carter." Libby groaned stupidly. "Ask her to come in."

The woman who entered was casually dressed. She had a plain face that radiated from the warmth of her smile. She reached out her hand, "Hello. I'm Martha Carter, coordinator for Volunteer Day Service. I've intended to stop in to see you for some time—to say thank you."

Libby returned her firm hand shake with a puzzled expression that made Miss Carter chuckle.

"I'm sorry, I do go on. I coordinate the delivery of hot meals to elderly people and I've been hearing about you and the banking-on-wheels service you provide to your customers. During holidays we have more volunteers than usual and that gives me a chance to call on people to express our thanks."

"Oh, I'm afraid it's all unofficial, in my spare time. The bank doesn't even know," Libby answered in alarm. Lewis Marvin had tried to warn her—now the bank would likely find out and she didn't know what that would do to her plan to persuade Stephen to include the home-banking program in Windsor Trust's services. "In fact, I doubt they'd approve."

"Please. I have no intention of causing you any problems with your employer," Martha Carter was quick to reassure her. "We just wanted to say that our entire organization is volunteer and, if you ever leave the bank, we'd love to have you."

"Thank you, Miss Carter. Those people also are very dear to me, but I'm afraid I haven't seen too much of them for the past two weeks since I've been sent downtown," she admitted guiltily.

"I know, but don't worry. Your manager has been filling in. As a matter-of-fact, he tells us he's about to retire and he's gotten so involved he's planning to volunteer to help us out, so a double thank you. But I do have a second mission.'' She reached down and lifted her shopping bag and pulled out a large, brightly-wrapped package.

''I don't understand . . . for me?''

''Oh, yes. And I'll have to tell you—I have one just like it.''

''What is it?''

''A friendship quilt made by Miss Lois and all the women in the retirement complex. I understand some of the men even wielded a needle. Happy New Year, Mrs. Spencer.'' Miss Carter smiled and said one more thank you before scurrying out.

Libby placed the shopping bag by her coatrack. She was ashamed. She'd been so caught up with the bank, and Stephen, and Will that she hadn't even called to check on the people she'd left behind.

She picked up the report she'd been working on but some of the enthusiasm was gone now. She felt so confused. The year was ending, a new one beginning, and for once she didn't look forward to it with enthusiasm. What would happen between her and Will? They'd been so busy since Christmas; Will with Tiger's arm, and she with the merger. Nothing had been said. Nothing had been decided.

''Libby.'' Stephen's voice startled her so that she dropped the sheath of papers she had been studying. They flew over the top of the desk and fanned across the floor like playing cards.

''Sorry, Stephen,'' she murmured, ''guess I'm a little edgy. What do you need?''

''That's a dangerous question, lady.''

''Please, Stephen, I'd rather you not talk like that

in the office." Libby's voice wavered and she bent down on one knee to retrieve the papers.

"Okay, no talk in the office, let's go for a walk, to lunch, to my apartment."

"Stephen!"

"No? I didn't really expect you to agree. But sooner or later, Libby, you're going to have to make up your mind about us."

"There is no us!" she snapped.

"I think there is. Will I see you tonight?"

"Yes, I suppose. Dixie told me you were invited to the party. I didn't know you were acquainted with Mr. Kendall."

"I'm not. Once I knew you were going to be there, I simply mentioned to your husband's friend, Pat, that I'd like to see the bank involved in local humanitarian affairs and he's expecting a big contribution."

"Yes, and speaking of humanitarian affairs, Stephen, I hope you are going to recommend that we keep the branch operations just as they are now. The branch banks are people-oriented. The bank could justify the kind of service we offer as Windsor Trust's way of serving the local community. Between the two of us, we ought to be able to think of some way to raise the deposit level at the neighborhood Peachtree Nationals, couldn't we?"

"I'm certainly willing to give it consideration, Libby. Why don't we spend some time discussing it. You know I value your opinions. We just don't seem to have time to discuss them here in the office."

Libby touched her fingertips to her temples, feeling the pounding of her head jar her thought process.

She was suddenly very tired. The strain of being near Stephen and trying to put up a wall between them was becoming harder and harder.

"What about it, Libby?"

"Please, Stephen, I'm afraid I'm getting a headache. It must be from studying all this fine print. I can't seem to understand what you're saying."

"Are you sure that's what's bothering you?" He walked slowly around the desk, catching her arm and lifting her up to face him. His eyes were wide with intensity. "I think it's me that has you upset. Look at me, Libby. It's time you quit avoiding the issue. Tell me that you don't want me to kiss you."

The feeling of the touch of his hands on her arms and the burning sensation where the pressure of his thigh held firm against her seemed to brand her and she sucked in her breath. "No," she whispered, and tried to pull her arms away.

But this time Stephen didn't stop. She was crushed against him, caught like a wild creature in a snare, with her predator looming over her, and she was helplessly paralyzed.

Her lips opened in wordless protest only to be captured by Stephen's mouth, not with gentleness, or the kind of loving nature she'd fantasized about, but with a wild urgency that drained and possessed. She felt hands enclose and lift her up against the demanding hardness of his body and she cried out as she tried to twist away. The force of his mouth ravished and plundered, while his hands possessed with a desperate need.

She tried once more to move away, her efforts only succeeding in urging him on, and her own body responded with a wildness that she hadn't been prepared for. What was happening to her? She was on fire. Her fingertips were frantic now to touch, and slipped between buttons to reach the hot bare skin below. What she might have imagined to be desire now paled in comparison and she knew for the first time in her life what it meant to be on fire.

When Stephen's hand touched her breast she felt the ripples splay out in ascending shock waves. Her nipples sprang erect and filled his hands, pushing against him, impatient now to stay inside the heat of his fingertips. His kisses fell now like hot-spangled beads, down her neck and across the top of her breasts, his lips vibrating against her hungrily.

"Ah, Libby," he tore his lips away from her, breathing now as heavily as she. "God, we're both on fire. You know it's true. You want this, too. When, how . . ."

"Oh, Stephen. I can't. I mean, I don't know." She heard herself falter and knew she was lost. She forced herself to be still. "I don't understand, Stephen. This isn't like me. I've never felt like this before. It's wrong. You confuse me." She felt tears well up and begin to slide down her face.

"God, Libby. You act like some innocent school girl playing games. I'm not a bad man and I'm not into game playing. I want you and I can give you what you want, too. Either get in this century or out of it." Stephen flung himself away from her and moved back toward the door, buttoning his shirt and rubbing himself tenderly as he forcibly willed the erection so obviously presenting itself to subside.

"I have to go upstairs for a meeting with the

board. I probably won't be back this afternoon. You think about what just happened. I don't play games. We want each other. I think we want each other very much. But I can't take any more I will, I won't. Either we see each other like two adults who want each other, or we stop right here. I'm too old for this kind of thing.''

Long after Stephen left, Libby huddled at her desk, holding her face in her hands. She tried to look at what had happened honestly, without the shame that colored the feelings she was experiencing. Her body seemed to respond to Stephen in every possible way. That she affected him the same was more than obvious. For the first time in her marriage, she was faced with something foreign to everything she'd planned in her life—another man.

It was stupid, she told herself, stupid to want this man to make love to her. A one-night stand years ago hadn't really been what she'd expected, neither had making love with Will. There must be something very wrong with her. All the butterflies and star bursts she was supposed to feel just weren't there except with Stephen, and she felt cheated. Was it all a lie? Did other women really feel all those things that men seemed to?

Was it Stephen who offered the promise of fulfillment, or was it simply the forbidden?

Maybe her idea of lovemaking—the pretty words and emotional release that spiraled into space—was all a lie. All a fantasy. But she knew that there was more to sex than she'd had. Stephen made her body burn like liquid fire and she wasn't so sure that she wanted to say no.

"Oh, Will," she whispered. "I'm so confused and I can't tell you. I can't even tell Dixie about this. I don't know if I'm strong enough to turn it down and I don't ever want to think about what will happen if I don't."

Libby didn't hear from Will. She didn't know if he was on duty, or if he'd just forgotten to call her. He hadn't been home for two nights. Tiger's arm was the center of his world for now and she felt like a terrible person for being jealous, but she was. What did that make her?

At lunchtime, when she picked up Will's tux at the shopping center, she passed the shop window displaying the evening gown she and Dixie had admired. It was still there, the bright red sequined gown. Dixie was right, it was lovely. It took only a moment to convince herself to try it on.

As she looked in the mirror she couldn't believe the transformation. It was an absolutely plain body-hugging gown with one bare shoulder, the other sleeve extending down the arm in a long vee hem that shimmered with every breath she took.

The floor-to-thigh slit showed her best asset, long slim legs that looked even more exotic when she added extra high rhinestone strappy heels.

She didn't know who she was dressing for. Will? He never noticed what she wore. Stephen? Maybe it was for herself. For once she wanted to look sophisticated and elegant and desirable. She gave the clerk her credit card and paid for the dress and the shoes, adding a pair of long dangling rhinestone earrings.

"I'm sorry, babe," he'd said when he finally called that afternoon. His voice sounded more tired than usual. She knew the strain between them had added to his fatigue. "But I'll be there tonight. The operation is beginning in a few minutes. I'll be home as soon as I'm sure everything is all right and Tiger is coming out of the anesthesia."

"Please, Will, don't forget. The party doesn't matter to me," she lied, "but Dixie is really going all out. And it is New Year's Eve," she ended wistfully. *And I have a slinky new dress, and . . . Oh, Will, I need you. For once in your life be there for me.*

Everything was building to a climax of sorts, Libby felt. Christmas had come and gone. The bank's merger was almost complete, and Tiger's surgery would be performed today. She couldn't avoid facing up to her feelings about Stephen and her commitment to Will . . . Everything seemed to be coming to an end, or maybe it wasn't the end but the new beginning. Libby turned on the radio to nice soft music that soothed as she laid out Will's clothes on one side of the bed and hers on the other. She filled the tub and added a gelatin capsule of bath oil and a handful of bubble bath, took off her clothes, and crawled in. The hot water began to relax her and she allowed herself a tinge of excitement at the night ahead.

Libby had never been to this kind of formal party before. Will's idea of a New Year's celebration was pizza and beer and taking in the latest movie. Once they'd even shared whistles and hats with a couple of winos who'd slipped into the local drive-in restaurant for a carefully hoarded cup of coffee and an hour of warmth. It had been fun, she admitted, but this evening was special. It was the kind of thing she'd always dreamed about and she was determined that nothing was going to spoil it. Will would be introduced as guest of honor and she'd be beside him. Finally, the water began to cool and Libby pulled the plug, rinsed out the tub, and toweled herself dry.

She rarely used her hot rollers, but tonight she plugged them in and turned back to the mirror to consider her hair. Tonight, she'd try something special. While her hair was setting—cooking as Will called it—she pulled on the metallic flesh-colored pantyhose and lacy wisps of underwear she'd chosen. No bra she decided wickedly, as if she needed one anyway.

Libby examined her nails critically. The slinky red dress demanded long red fingernails. What she had were short clear fingernails. Somewhere in the back of the bathroom drawer she had a package of false fingernails she had bought on a whim when she and Dixie were in college. She'd never tried them. Will would probably laugh. Thirty minutes later, she had glued them on, trimmed them to shape, and filed them smooth. After a few awkward attempts, she managed to cover them reasonably well with a deep red polish almost the same color as her gown.

Slipping her arms into her housecoat, she wandered restlessly back into the living room, determined to give them enough time to dry so that she wouldn't lose one at the party. The living room looked drab now that the Christmas tree was down. She'd come home from work one afternoon and the tree was down and all the ornaments put away. She'd felt left out somehow that Will had done it without her. Then she remembered all the years she'd done it without him.

"How about that, babe?" he'd asked, pleased that he'd surprised her with unexpected help. She hadn't wanted to look in the boxes. No telling how he'd put them away.

It was growing late now and Libby couldn't help wondering when Will would get home. She put away the friendship quilt, laying her face against it for a moment, marveling at the tiny stitches so lovingly sewn. She wandered restlessly back to the bathroom and began to work on her face. First a moisturizer, then a base coat of beige color with a cherry blush worked delicately in around the cheekbones. A pearl-silver eye shadow across her lids was followed by a shimmering, glittery film that would enhance her dark eyes and give an elegant sheen to her face. It had taken her longer than usual because of the awkwardness of adjusting to the fingernails. By the time she looked up, she realized that Will had come in and was watching her, an odd flicker of interest in his eyes.

"Is this a party tonight, or an audition for a Las Vegas chorus line? I don't know if I can keep up with such a classy lady."

What started as an unkind remark ended as something of a compliment and Libby didn't quite know how to answer Will. The last thing she wanted to do tonight was to say something to spoil the mood of the evening. She finally looked back at herself in the mirror, head full of rollers, and began to laugh. "A

Halloween party is a better destination for me at the moment."

Libby turned to leave the bathroom, not anxious to submit all her painstaking efforts to the steam from Will's shower. "I'll let you have the bathroom while I get my dress on. I'll comb my hair while you're dressing." She began to remove her robe, paused and looked at Will who was still watching. "Oh, I forgot, how is Tiger? Was the operation a success?"

"Yes, at least the attachment of the arm was. He was still asleep when I left. We won't really know how successful the implant is until he wakes up and tries to move it." Will began removing his clothes, dropping them momentarily to the floor, then reaching down to pick them up with a little smirk that said he knew she was watching and he was doing the proper thing.

"You know, Lib," he called from the shower, "he's a tough little kid. Can you imagine being on the other side of the world, away from your family and everything you knew, facing such an unknown?"

Will wrapped himself in a towel and padded back into the bedroom. "I don't know if I have that kind of courage."

"I know," Libby agreed, pulling the side zipper closed. "He's very brave."

Will let out a long audible breath. "Damn, Libby. What kind of dress is that? It makes you look like, like . . ." Will stuttered in bewilderment as his eyes took in the new Libby removing her rollers as she walked into the bathroom.

"Like what, Will? Do I look like a woman whose husband is the guest of honor? Or do I look like a junior executive in the upper echelons of the banking world?"

"Uh, I don't know, Libby. I guess that kind of question is a little out of my line, but you certainly look—different." He stood drying himself absently, his eyes following her body movements as she lifted her arms over her head to remove the rollers. "Are you sure that's what the other women are wearing?"

"No," Libby said, matter-of-factly. "I'm not sure what the other women are wearing. I'm only sure of what I'm wearing, and tonight," she turned and looked directly at him, daring him to question her presentability further, "tonight, I'm wearing this."

"And this funeral director's outfit you have here is what I'm wearing, I suppose." Will shook his head, looked back at Libby and began to dress. He slipped long legs into black trousers, put his arms into the white-tucked shirt, and looked helplessly at the absence of buttons.

"Libby, I'm sorry, but I don't have any idea how this shirt works, can you give me a hand?"

"Honestly, Will, for someone who can figure what makes a machine reprint the Bill of Rights from memory, why can't you figure out how button studs work?" She fastened the studs in the shirt and at the cuffs, fastened the vest, and snapped the bow tie into place. She had stepped back and turned to admire the elegant couple, she could see in the mirror when the phone rang.

Libby knew before Will answered it that she should have reached for the phone herself. "Yes, this is Dr. Spencer. What? You're sure? Yes, you did absolutely right. I'll be right down."

"Will," Libby warned, "you're not going anywhere, not tonight. You promised."

"I'm sorry, Libby. It's Tiger. He's having a hard time coming out of the anesthesia and they're afraid he's going to damage his arm. They need me to come and help calm him down, just for a short time. I promise I won't stay long. I'll meet you at Dixie's. Libby, I promise. I'll be there in plenty of time."

Libby watched him slide his feet into the shiny black-patent rented shoes, put on the satin-lapeled dinner coat, and give his hair a quick comb before filling his pockets and heading for the door. "I'll take your car, that'll save time. You call a cab." His quick kiss never hit her lips and the scalding words she bit back became an unswallowable lump in her throat.

Of course, he had to go to the child. She could understand that. The poor little fellow, waking up in another country, in pain and afraid. She wouldn't have expected Will to do anything else. He was concerned about the boy. Her thoughts were uncharitable and hurtful. And she was thoroughly ashamed.

More pain. More guilt. Libby felt tears well up in her eyes. She wouldn't cry. She simply wouldn't cry and spoil her make-up. She'd just comb out her hair, retouch her lips, and wait for a cab. Dixie wouldn't have to know that Will wasn't there. He'd be there in plenty of time. He promised. He knew how much this evening meant to her.

If necessary, facing Dixie with the news that Will was late wouldn't be so terrible. Still, Libby worried. What would all those possible contributors think? What would Dixie's father think? When the cab arrived, Libby squared her shoulders and gave the driver the address. She wouldn't worry. Will would be there in plenty of time. After all, no matter how he felt about attending, he'd told the head of the department that he would be there. It was for his project. He'd be there. He promised.

The driveway to Dixie's house was lined with ice-white lights glittering in the trees like frozen tears. Libby shivered, pulled her velvet cape up around her neck, and stepped out of the cab.

She was late. She didn't know whether or not she could face an entire evening wandering around without Will. When the butler opened the door, he smiled stiffly, recognizing Libby from her past visits.

"Don't announce me, Roger, I'll just leave my cape and take myself in. Dr. Spencer is parking the car and he'll be along shortly."

Why did I tell Roger such a lie? He doesn't know and doesn't even care. She was nervous, very nervous, and she was trying very hard not to show it.

The sound of more guests entering behind her spurred her into action and she followed the sound of music and muted conversation. The combination living room–study had been opened, allowing both rooms to become one and it was completely full of people. Libby slipped inside, grateful for the anonymity of the crowd. She took a glass from a passing waiter and found a corner seat near the door where she could watch for Will and see without being seen.

The sudden burst of self-confidence that had boosted her when she put on her dress was gone and she huddled miserably in her corner, successfully avoiding the attempts of several unattached men to engage her in conversation. Her eyes mentally surveyed the crowd. She couldn't see Stephen anywhere. She was both glad and disappointed. Could she introduce Stephen to Will?

"Will, I'd like you to meet my former lover. It wasn't you who took away my virginity like you thought. It was Stephen Colter, my boss, the man who wants to make love to me."

Stop it, she told herself miserably. It wasn't going at all like she'd planned. Instead of having men drawn to her sophisticated, desirable presence, she was sitting in the corner behind a rubber plant, ill at ease and getting slightly tipsy from the cocktails she kept replacing her empty glass with.

"Libby, what are you doing over here?" Dixie strode across the room, pulling Libby to her feet. "Where's Will?"

"Uh, he's around some place, Dixie. You know men, find another man to talk to and they're gone." Libby knew she was chattering shrilly, and she knew that Dixie sensed her discomfort.

"Libby, you look absolutely gorgeous," Dixie reassured her. "I knew that dress would do wonders for you. Is Will pleased with the glamorous creature he's out with tonight?"

"Surprised is a better word. He thought I was trying out to be a Las Vegas showgirl."

"Well, if you were, you'd certainly make it. I never realized what good-looking legs you have. Come along, let's circulate." Libby was suddenly a part of Dixie's effervescence and she was content to loll around in the background as Dixie made her way through the growing crowd of people.

Where was Will? It was almost time for dinner. If he missed dinner, his place would be conspicuously empty. What would she say? Libby looked around the room, filled with influential people, her spirits dropping by the minute. She could see Governor Holder talking to Susan Wells, star reporter for the *Times*. Over near the window was Mayor Black and the news director for WYAP, unaffectionately referred to by Will as Yap, and Spinner Sutton, the ex-football player and millionaire businessman, was holding court near the bar. It had to be the most stunning New Year's Eve party in history, all planned to honor her husband and the work he was doing at the hospital, and Will hadn't shown up.

"All right, Libby, love. Thanks to Daddy we've assembled everyone with money and influence in the state. A few words about all Will's kids without arms and legs and they'll pledge enough money to buy them two each and Will will think you're the best thing since sliced bread." Dixie paused to offer her cheek to a matronly steel-haired woman towing a small balding man behind.

"Lovely party, Dixie. Thank you so much for having us."

"So glad you could come. Have you met Libby Spencer? No? Babs Winkle meet Libby Spencer. Get yourself a party hat over by the bar, Babs."

After Libby had made the appropriate response, Dixie gave the woman a hug and moved past her, whispering to Libby, "Her husband is chairman of the board of Solomon's, the company that just bought all those lovely department stores. Let her put her name on Will's artificial limbs and she's good for a dozen feet, at least.''

"Oh, Dixie. You shouldn't talk like that. Someone might overhear you." Libby was overwhelmed. Dixie had outdone herself and Libby was dreadfully uncomfortable. She wasn't at all sure she belonged here, not with all these people. She had thought this was going to be the most exciting evening in her life, that she might impress Stephen with her ability to mingle with the rich and famous.

She knew that this was his kind of life and these were his kind of people. He'd said she deserved designer dresses and penthouses. But all she wanted to do was run. She and Dixie circled the room speaking and being spoken to until they were back at the den again.

"It's almost time to hit the pocketbooks, Libby. Everyone is here except the man who needs to be introduced. Where is Will Spencer hiding?"

"Oh, Dixie," Libby wailed. "I don't know. He didn't want to come and then the university told him he had to. He was very angry."

"So, where is he? As tall as he is, there's no way he can hide, even in this crowd, and I haven't seen him yet."

"He didn't come, Dixie. When we were dressing, he got a call that Tiger, that's the little boy who spent Christmas with us, was having a bad time after his operation. Will left to go to the hospital for a few minutes to quiet him down. He never came back."

"Do you mean you had to come alone? No wonder you're miserable."

The band had stopped playing and was giving a

loud drum roll to introduce Dixie's father, now stepping briskly to the platform.

"Welcome my friends. Before the lot of us are given an opportunity to set aside all our sins and weaknesses with a fresh new year to mess up, I'd like to talk to you about redeeming yourself. My daughter has come up with a project that might allow you to do just that. Dixie? Where are you? Come and explain and introduce the genius that started it. Dixie?"

The crowd began to look around and Libby slid helplessly back away from Dixie as far as possible. How could she face all those people, explain Will's absence? It was too much. She'd already been hovering near the door for the last hour with a smile pasted on her face. She sensed someone behind her now and knew that if she didn't get away she would embarrass Dixie by crying. Her tears would spoil any chance of raising money for Will. She took a desperate look at the question on Dixie's face, shook her head, and whirled around—straight into the arms of Stephen Colter.

Libby struggled to loosen the pressure of his hands on her shoulders as she heard Dixie behind her greeting her friends and guests. "I'm afraid our guest of honor isn't here . . ."

"Oh, Stephen," Libby said, "take me away from here. Please!"

NINE

Will hadn't wanted to leave Tiger after surgery. The operation had gone well. The biggest worry, connecting the ligaments and muscles to the computer in the arm, had worked even better than they expected. Will had dressed out, and assisted in surgery, something he rarely did.

When they rolled Tiger back to recovery, Will had been surprised at the depth of his feelings for the child. He'd never felt he had time for a child, but he admitted, if only to himself, that he'd miss Tiger when he was gone. Tiger was waking very slowly and Will knew that he was already later leaving the hospital than he'd promised Libby. He couldn't ignore his irritation that Libby had interfered in his work by obligating him to appear at Dixie's New Year's Eve party. He was sure that some of Libby's recent dissatisfaction came from her association with Dixie.

"Go to the party," the head of research had directed when he joined Will in the recovery room. "It's good public relations."

171

"I'd rather spend my free time here," Will protested. "Tiger may wake up afraid."

"We have already assigned a nurse he's accustomed to to stay with him." When Will started to argue, Dr. Pullen raised his hand and shook his head. "Now, Will, if we can spend our free time operating on your charity cases, you can spend some of yours in a little politicking. Who knows, you might actually pick up some donations for your project."

So Will had given up and headed home, resigned to dreading the evening ahead. When the hospital had called him back, he'd been glad, though the disappointed look in Libby's eyes had stayed with him all the way back downtown. That he might have set himself up to be called was something he tried not to think about.

On his return his lengthy strides covered the hospital corridor like a long-distance runner, neither seeing nor acknowledging the greetings of fellow workers along the way until he reached the child's room.

Tiger was moving about, moaning softly, looking small and very vulnerable in the high-railed bed.

"Dr. Spencer," the efficient young nurse whispered softly, "I'm glad you're here. He's been calling for you. We've been waiting until you arrived before sedating him again."

"Hey, Tiger?"

At the sound of Will's voice the boy's eyes flew open. "Will?" The frightened little voice quivered in relief. "Tiger's new arm hurt."

"Yes, I know, Tiger." Will's quiet words and gentle touch stilled the child. "We knew it would, but you must be very quiet." Will pulled up the straight-backed chair and sat down opposite Tiger, still rubbing the well arm patiently. "I'll stay with you until you sleep."

When the nurse came back in with the hypodermic needle, Tiger's face screwed up in protest until he felt the pressure of Will's hand tighten on his arm. He quickly bit back the impending protest, glanced at Will, and held out his arm for the shot.

"He'll sleep now," the nurse said as she administered the injection. "He just seemed to be so upset that we followed your orders and called."

"He expected me to be here when he woke up," Will explained. "I think I'll just sit a while, if you'll stay for a moment while I run down to the car and get my reading material."

"Weren't you going out?" she asked curiously.

"Oh," Will looked down at the fancy black tuxedo and the black patent shoes and pleated white shirt. "Yes, but it's a dinner dance. I'll just skip the cocktail party and the dinner."

With any luck, he decided as he took the service elevator to the garage, he'd miss most of it. Just so long as he put in an appearance, he would make Libby and his boss, Bill Pullen, happy.

Other people didn't understand Will's avoidance of people and he found it hard to explain. It wasn't that he didn't like people, he did. But he never could remember names. He didn't watch TV and the normal conversation about golf and the stock market just seemed like inane chatter. His lack of interest made him appear stuffy and out of place and he grew impatient with wasting time.

The book he had brought along had slipped under

the car seat and Will rummaged about in the dark until his fingers reached it. He pulled it out and slipped it under his arm. A soft light had been placed by the chair near Tiger's head while he'd been gone.

"Let me know when you leave and I'll come back and stay with him." The night nurse excused herself and Will settled down, watching Tiger's already closed eyes and even breathing.

He'd just sit here for a little while and make sure Tiger stayed quiet. Then maybe he'd drop back later and check again. The longer he delayed arriving at Dixie's party, the less time he'd have to stay. Libby would probably have a better time without him anyway.

Will opened the book to the page marked by a folded slip of paper and began to read the paragraphs in the penciled-in brackets.

Don't be timid. If, after arousing the man in your life, his lovemaking still isn't satisfying you, it's up to you to let him know what pleases you.

"What the . . .?"

Will quickly flipped back to the front of the book. *Secrets to a More Exciting Sex Life* by Angel Harper. Libby must have left her book in her car, the same book she'd been hugging that night he'd put her to bed. His first inclination was mild disgust, surprise even, that Libby would waste her time reading something sensational like this. Then he thought back to the book she'd playfully wrapped as a Christmas joke. What had it been called, something about how to love your lover? He not only hadn't looked at it, he didn't even know where it was.

The situation was bizarre and he didn't know quite

what to make of Libby's odd behavior. His analytical mind overruled his natural distaste for such sensationalism and he began to read Angel's secrets.

When Will came to the chapter on rekindling a disinterested husband's interest, he sat straight up. Ms. Angel Harper had an entire section of titillating suggestions, beginning interestingly enough with wrapping oneself in plastic and greeting your unsuspecting lover at the front door. He skimmed the rest in utter disbelief, eternally grateful that Libby hadn't chosen the great whipped-cream lick-off, until he reached the last chapters, dealing seriously with the physical aspects of making love.

How to and What to Expect When You Do it was titled. It was ridiculous to think that this silly woman had anything to say or should be listened to when she did. Yet, he read on, telling himself that he really ought to have some idea of how Libby's mind was working now.

When Will flipped the book closed at last, he sat staring at the curious shadowed circle of light on the wall behind Tiger's bed. Maybe it was the power of suggestion, but it looked like Libby's breast, small and soft, and he felt incredibly sad. What a fool he'd been, taking on the world's problems like some kind of crusader and leaving the most important part of his own world so ignored that she bought how-to books to entice her own husband to make love to her.

Libby, with brown eyes that flashed and snapped, changing as they revealed her inner moods so beautifully, until her own impenetrable shade came down and everything went all efficient and organized to hide her feelings. She would have made a good nurse, he thought. Hell, she'd have made a good doctor.

Will smiled, remembering Libby wrapped in cellophane. Despite his blundering reaction, she *had* aroused him. But he hadn't had time to pursue physical desire, not then, and he'd simply called out his very practiced doctor's mask to close out his feelings and once again it had worked, too well.

What had happened? Will cleared his throat angrily. When had Libby become so dissatisfied that she needed a book to reach him? How had they both become so expert at closing out their real feelings? Had it been Tiger that had brought their lack of communication out in the open? No, it had started long before that, in the very beginning. His work had simply taken over every waking moment. He'd been in control there. With Libby, he'd never admitted it before, but he'd been less certain in his actions.

She'd never complained and he'd never asked if she was—if their lovemaking was good for her. And eventually he'd become used to their routine. Libby simply became a part of him. She'd always been the best part of his success. She had kept things running smoothly so that he could concentrate on important things and when everything went right, she'd been his recreation, his dessert, his reward. But what had he been to her?

You've been a fool, Will told himself bitterly. A blind, insensitive fool. The book made more sense than he wanted to admit. It wasn't the silly things Angel Harper advocated, but the serious suggestions on the more dog-eared pages at the back, that had crashed in on him, with startling clarity. You, a doctor of all people, a doctor who is supposed to understand the workings of a woman's body. You have a wife whose dissatisfaction is destroying her life and she can't tell her own husband. It was all becoming so clear.

Will stood, suddenly rigid with an unnamed fear. He had to reach Libby, quickly before it was too late. The realization bit through him like the shiny blade of one of his scalpels. He remembered Pat had mentioned seeing Libby at lunch with her new boss, Simon, Sam, no . . . Stephen something or other. He'd thought at the time that Pat had been describing them at lunch in a rather curious tone.

Come to think of it, he didn't recall Libby mentioning a new boss. And a downtown lunch at the Top of the World was certainly out of character. Then there was the matter of the pink roses that came with no signature. Will felt his heart compress and his breath begin to burn his lungs from being held.

Will glanced over at Tiger, sleeping quietly, and down at his watch. Damn, it was late, maybe too late. Maybe he'd blown everything. He stopped briefly at the nurses' station, told them he was leaving, and tore down the steps to the car.

He needed to get to this party and make an appearance. He needed to go through the motions, do it right, so that Libby would be pleased. He'd made fun of it, without stopping to realize that it was an important attempt on Libby's part to involve herself in his work.

"Raise money?" he'd said. "More likely an excuse to spend money on new clothes or see and be seen.'' And he hadn't stopped there. "Any money left over may be invested in medical research so long as the donor gets plenty of publicity and documented tax records.''

The distance between the hospital and Dixie's father's home was covered in record time. Explaining his absence to Libby wasn't something he looked forward to and he was reconciled to her quick hurt look, followed by a stiff upper lip and busy hands. He'd seen it before and he winced to know how thoughtlessly he'd dismissed it.

It wasn't until he reached the front door that he caught himself and paused to plan his course of action. He had so many things to straighten out, beginning with this party. He ran his fingers through his hair the way he always did when he was ill at ease or preoccupied, straightened his tie and hoped he looked the part of a potential Nobel Prize winner. Then he rang the bell.

The butler who opened the door glared accusingly at Will and stepped aside, obviously unsure whether or not this wrinkled, unkempt guest was expected.

"Yes?''

"I'm looking for my wife . . . eh, Libby Spencer.''

"All our guests are at dinner, sir. If you'll wait here.''

Still at dinner? That was even worse. Now he'd have to find Libby in a room full of people he didn't know and his need to talk to her would have to wait until later.

"Will?'' Dixie Kendall appeared in the doorway, a frown on her face. "Where ever have you been? Libby has been beside herself.''

"Sorry, Dixie, I've been tied up at the hospital and couldn't get away. No, that's a lie, Dixie. I didn't want to come and I delayed as much as possible. Where is Libby? I need to talk to her."

"She's gone, Will." Dixie stammered. "You weren't here and she left." Dixie hesitated a moment as though making up her mind, then spoke again. "Come into the library, Will, I'd better talk to you."

Dixie closed the door behind them and leaned against it. "I don't want to interfere, Will. I know you've never had a high opinion of me, but whether you realize it or not, I'm very fond of Libby and you."

"Please go on, Dixie. I think I need to hear what you are worried about saying."

"Libby was more upset than I realized. She didn't tell us you weren't here with her. When Daddy was ready to introduce you and you hadn't come, she left."

"But how? I had her car."

"Oh, Will, I'm probably going to regret saying this for the rest of my life, but I've never been known for tact." She swallowed hard and looked at the grim expression on Will's face, then lifted her head, let out a long breath and spoke. "Will, Libby didn't leave alone. She left with her boss, Stephen Colter."

Dixie's words fell across him like an icy wind and he felt himself blanch and reel crazily, while her words sank in. "I don't believe it," he whispered, knowing all the while he did. Hadn't he practically pushed her toward someone else? He rubbed his eyebrows with thumb and forefinger, rolling the skin on his forehead up into his hairline.

No, he told himself. You won't go after her. Libby isn't one of those women who run away. She'll come back. Even if you found her, what could you do or say that she would believe? Reverting to his analytical approach, the one he used to lay the groundwork for solving the most impossible problem, he said without realizing that he'd spoken aloud, "If you expect a logical result, you must lay the proper foundation."

"True, but hardly the answer I'd expect," Dixie replied in puzzled annoyance, "considering the information I just gave you."

"Dixie, I'm not going to follow Libby. What would I say? That I'm not going to neglect her anymore, that I'll do better? My track record puts me in last place on all counts. No, I'm going to do what she wanted me to do and hope it isn't too late." He took Dixie's arm, opened the door, and clicked his heels together smartly. "I believe you have a group of people looking for a place to put their money? Lead me to them."

Will escorted a thoroughly confused Dixie into the dining room and took his place behind the empty spot adjacent to where Dixie was sitting, stopping a moment to nod at the guests who had paused in hushed speculation. The waiters were already removing the desert plates as Dixie began.

"Ladies and gentlemen, our guest of honor would like a moment to explain himself and his tardy arrival. I'd like you to meet one of the nicest, most dedicated people I know, Dr. Will Spencer."

Will began to speak, explaining in his usual fumbling, sincere way about his work, about Tiger and the other patients whose arms and legs had been replaced by experimental computer-operated limbs that had become more and more lifelike. He spoke of his visions for the future, of his dreams to make paralyzed limbs move by inserting computer-programed modules that would issue commands disrupted by severed nerves and muscles that no longer received directions from the brain. He looked around in pleasant surprise at the attentive expressions of dinner guests who looked as though they would be far more comfortable at bridge tables and playing billiards.

"Do you mean you've actually permanently attached a lifelike artificial arm to a child's body?"

Will recognized the questioner as Susan Wells, the news reporter for WYAP.

"It's not one of those strap on things?"

"Yes, we have attached it directly to the body, though the idea isn't new, and it isn't really permanent. It will have to be changed as the child grows. What makes this unique is that nerves and muscles in the shoulder feed the computer which directs the arm to respond in a very lifelike manner."

"How soon will you be able to adapt this to legs? Can you use the same principal to give movement to paraplegics?"

"We hope so, in time, so long as the limbs have not atrophied from lack of use for too long a period of time."

The questions went on and Will began to reevaluate Dixie and her friends. Libby had been right. The idea had been good. Publicity from the news media, not for himself, but for the project was what they so desperately needed to raise funds.

Mr. Kendall finally called a stop to the barrage of questions and made a generous donation to the university research program to continue Will's work. In no time, more money had been pledged than Will ever imagined, and the success and good wishes were heady.

"I don't believe this," Will muttered in amazement as he and Dixie threaded through the crowd of well-wishers. "There are so many worthwhile, outstretched hands, why fill mine?"

"Because they recognize an honest, dedicated man with the kind of vision they all wish they had."

"Do you realize that I had my picture taken with both the Mayor and Spinner Sutton? For once I'm right where Libby wanted us to be and she isn't here." Will turned to Dixie in disappointment. "She didn't come back, did she?"

"No, not yet."

"I've been here over an hour, Dixie. She isn't coming." He hadn't realized until now how desperately he'd wanted her to return. She'd never done anything that wasn't proper and acceptable. From the time they had gotten married she had her own blueprint of what she expected their life to be and she hadn't deviated—until tonight.

"Maybe she's already at home, Will. You know Libby, she's probably pulled out her oldest nightgown and is making cocoa."

"I hope you are right, and thank you. I've been

very wrong about you . . . and a lot of things, Dixie. You're a good friend to Libby and me.''

"Wait, Will, it's still over an hour until midnight. Wait here, just a minute." Dixie slipped back through the crowd, disappeared briefly, then reappeared holding something behind her back. "Take this, Will, and when you get home, toast the New Year with Libby. Tell her I was wrong. Love is for yesterday, tomorrow, and *always*.''

"The card on the flowers, from him."

Dixie looked startled. "No, not from him. I sent the roses, Will. It was part of a plan that Libby and I cooked up to make you jealous. She thought that you didn't care about her anymore.''

The flowers weren't from another man. Will clung to the magnum of champagne, and to Dixie's words, all the way home, up the steps and into the dark apartment. Libby wasn't there.

He turned on the small lamp in the entrance way, and set the bottle of champagne on the kitchen counter while he found the only bucket they had large enough to fill with ice and still hold the champagne. In the back of the cabinet he located two long-stemmed crystal glasses and some lace paper napkins. The silver engraved tray they'd gotten from the neighbors at home for a wedding gift would hold the glasses and napkins. He carried them back into the living room and placed them on the floor.

Next, he brought in the bucket filled with ice and champagne. But somehow, a green plastic bucket spoiled the romantic mood he was trying to create. A second trip to the kitchen brought out the roll of tin foil and a few minutes later, Will's champagne bucket was silver. The only whistle he could find was a silver policeman's whistle that he'd bought for Tiger. But what the hell, it made noise. A plastic bag full of cut-up funny papers made confetti and he was ready. He didn't have funny hats, but funny wasn't on his list. He turned on "Guy Lombardo's New Year's Eve Party" and sat down on the floor to watch and wait.

The party switched back and forth between the network late-night talk show, the party, and Times Square. There was a time when Will couldn't have visualized himself at a party like that, wearing outlandish paper hats and dancing unselfconsciously before the world. There was a slim, dark-haired girl dressed in a pale-blue dress that reminded him of Libby, the Libby he'd become accustomed to in years past.

Will removed his jacket and vest and tossed them across the room. Libby certainly hadn't looked like that tonight. The bright sequined gown she'd been wearing was provocative and eye-catching. It had shimmered when she'd moved and he could see long slim legs through the slit in the side of the dress. She'd looked vibrant and alive and exciting, and he'd left her, almost surely cleared the way for another man to take what he'd so carelessly ignored. God, he wanted her to come home.

It was eleven-fifteen now and still no Libby. Will resigned himself to the fact that she wasn't coming and opened the bottle of champagne. He didn't know too much about alcohol. For the most part, he simply hadn't had time to learn. The only night he'd ever gone out with the boys was the night before he'd come back to make love to Libby.

He still couldn't believe how cavalier he'd been in turning her down when she'd offered herself to him. He'd been an ass. The next week had been the most miserable in his life. When he finally decided that he'd never be able to concentrate again until he'd made things right with Libby, he'd gone out drinking until he'd got up enough courage to do the thing she wanted—make mad passionate love to her. Then he'd forgotten his misery. Once she belonged to him, he'd gone on with his life without a thought for her.

The way things stood now, Libby had no reason to believe that the pattern would change. He'd made the first move, the party, and she hadn't been there to see it. It was hard, very hard to face his actions as a man. If things were going to work out, if their lives were to reach a new dimension, he must approach his problems honestly.

He'd emptied his glass and refilled it as the TV party grew noisier and noisier. He'd been fooling himself six years ago and what made it even worse, he'd continued to fool himself in all the years since. Their marriage was a sham, a shell. It had taken a foolish woman's book to make him see what every other red-blooded *Playboy*-reading man had known since the age of fifteen.

Will Spencer was a failure. Love wasn't enough for the modern, well-informed woman. They were saying so in every magazine, movie, and conversation. They also wanted old-fashioned lust. Tenderness and kindness were comforting but, sexually,

Libby deserved more. He poured another glass of champagne.

Will Spencer might win a Nobel Prize for his work, but in bed with Libby the only award he'd likely get was the booby prize. But if Will was anything, he was thorough. Once his mind settled on a problem, he solved it. Now he leaned back against the couch, closed his eyes, and planned the seduction of Libby Spencer.

TEN

"Get me out of here, Stephen, please," Libby repeated, feeling the eyes of every guest in the room on her.

A sturdy arm slipped around her and supported her out the door, past the startled butler and into the warm silver sportscar waiting at the door to be parked.

Stephen closed the door behind Libby and moved around to the driver's side. He took the handkerchief tucked in his breast pocket and pressed it into Libby's hand. Stephen drove rapidly away, into the cold gray night, while Libby huddled in the corner sobbing noisily as though all the pent-up tears in a lifetime flowed unchecked.

Sometime later, the car pulled into a dimly-lit driveway and stopped in the shadow of a large tree. Stephen left the engine running, flicked on his lighter, and lit a small aromatic cigar. He sat smoking quietly until Libby began to calm herself.

As the tears dried up, Libby leaned her head

against the velvet softness of the carseat and waited for Stephen to speak.

He didn't.

After a time, he opened the car door, ground out the cigar, and came around to her side, lifting her once more in arms that rippled with solid strength. This time he didn't voice the question, he no longer waited for her answer, she'd already given it.

The thick carpet muffled every sound in the building's lobby, and Libby had the feeling that she was off to the side, watching herself move with no conscious control. There was an eerie weightless feeling about her body. This wasn't her, this was the Libby she'd imagined in fantasies, moving through a dream.

The elevator door slid silently open and Stephen stepped inside still holding her. A dim whirl and blinking light said they were moving up. Up? Where?

"Stephen?"

"Hush, don't talk."

The elevator doors opened once more and Stephen let her feet slide to the floor, still holding her close with his right arm, while reaching for his keys with his left hand. Libby stumbled slightly and he quickly recaptured her body, pulling her even closer as he opened the door and they moved inside. Dimly, she saw plush navy and silver furnishings, chrome and glass, and the soft shimmering of candlelight.

A sudden chill rippled her body and she began to shake. Her legs were limp and she swayed. She didn't understand what was happening.

"Stephen, I . . ."

"Libby, it's all right," Stephen put both arms

around her and held her, comforting, running his palms across her shoulders in a gentle soothing motion.

"What's wrong with me, Stephen?" Her voice sounded strange and distant as though someone else was speaking.

"Stress, you're in a mild state of shock, Libby, emotional shock. The body reacts to stress and yours is sending protests to your brain. When the brain fails to accept the message, the body blanks out. In olden times, the heroine fainted."

"But I'm so cold."

He swung her up into his arms once more and carried her through the living room, down a hallway, into the dark room at the end of the corridor.

"Now, just stand here for a moment. We need to get you warm. You rushed out of the party without a coat. It's freezing out there. I think we just might have snow."

She felt him reach behind her; his hands, first on her back, then moving around to the side. She realized belatedly that he was unzipping her dress. "No," she pleaded. "Please no."

"Be still, Libby. I'm not going to make love to you. Not unless you want me to, and I think you want me to. I think you want me to very much."

She felt his fingers feathering her backbone as he slid her dress down her body; a fiery jolt of heat radiating outward from the trail he'd followed. She had to stop him she told herself as he laid her back on the bed. Bed? "No, Stephen, I don't want . . ."

"Want, Libby," he said huskily. "You don't know what you want. One minute it's Will, then your career, then the next minute it's me."

His hands curled silkily around her shoulders and across her breasts and she felt her body simmering with a thousand little pinpoints of heat.

He was covering her with blankets now and she lay ramrod stiff shivering beneath them. "You sound so angry, Stephen," she said between chattering teeth. "What have I done?"

"Done? You really don't know, do you?"

She felt him move away and found being alone was worse than having him near. "Stephen?"

"I'm here. Drink this."

"What is it? You aren't drugging me, are you?" She shrank back into the pillow.

"What a child you are, Libby, a hot-blooded woman-child. When are you going to grow up and stop trying to be daddy's little girl? Drink. It's nothing but brandy, to stimulate you."

"Stimulate me, why?"

"To warm you up, make you stop shivering. This has nothing to do with sex, Libby. God knows, sexual stimulation is one thing I don't think you need." He was losing patience now and Libby lifted her head and gulped down the burning liquid.

"Good, now just lie there for a moment and listen to me."

"Only if you stop being so mad at me. I like the Stephen who sends roses better."

"Roses? What roses? I haven't sent you flowers, though I will if that's what you want. I thought we were past playing those courting games."

"And the little ivory unicorn? You didn't send it either?"

"No, but I'll buy you a platinum unicorn with a

diamond horn if that's what you want. Libby, I'm wealthy and I'm generous.''

Stephen hadn't sent the flowers or the unicorn. Will certainly hadn't. Then who? Dixie! Making Will think she had a lover had been Dixie's idea. From the first her dream had been a lie. Libby began to laugh. Maybe Dixie's plan had worked.

The brandy was rippling through her and with the heat of the blankets her chills were beginning to subside. And with the subsiding of her jangling nerve endings, her mind began to clear. What was she doing here? What did she really want? She took a long level look at the stranger with the puzzled expression on his face, the man who had come back into her life at a time when she was most vulnerable.

Stephen Colter was handsome, successful, and very attentive. He knew how to make a woman feel desirable and wanted. But was she attracted to him because she really wanted him, or was it because he made her come to life sexually in a way that Will never had? She knew that Stephen was experienced, that under his touch she would respond and she was tempted. But more than the physical, he made her feel important. A team, that's what he was promising. A future with a career that beckoned to the ambition in her and a physical relationship that promised the kind of glorious lovemaking she so desperately wanted.

''I do want you, Stephen. You and I both know I'm not sophisticated enough to conceal it. But what do you want from me? All the promises of advancement at the bank, a beautiful life, I don't understand.

Be specific now. I want to know what you expect and what you're offering.''

"Well," he smiled, running a finger down the side of her face, down her neck into the hollow between her breasts, a pleased expression crinkling his eyes when she didn't draw away. "We're good together, you and I. Our minds work well together. The kind of life I lead doesn't lend itself to the normal marriage and homelife that would satisfy most men. I like the idea of you coming with me. I've never been able to forget that night we spent together and I still want you."

Libby closed her eyes. She wanted to hear the words, but she couldn't face him as he told her how he felt.

"You know you were, believe it or not, the first virgin I ever made love to. As a matter-of-fact, you're the only one and that makes you very special. I thought, after *your* branch of the bank closes, I'd see to it that you were made my personal assistant. That way, we could move between all the corporate holdings without question. That's what I'm offering you, Libby. We'll see the world, you and I."

She felt as if her heart had just stopped beating. *After your branch of the bank closes.* "I see," she said, taking his hand away from her breast and placing it back on his knee. "You knew all along that the branch was being closed. All that talk about interceding for all those old people was a lie. There won't be any traveling banking service, will there?"

"No, that's not true, not entirely," he said seriously. "I did consider it. But sentiment and dollars and cents just don't match. Your branch was the only weak link in the chain and I learned a long time ago that if you want to get to the top, you've got to be tough. I did get them an automatic teller.''

"Oh, Stephen," she said in disgust. "Those old people don't know about bank cards and machines. They'd be perfect targets to be mugged." She pulled back the cover and threw her feet over the edge of the bed.

"Where are you going?" he demanded as she stepped back into the dress and slid it over her body. "No more games, Libby, you came with me. You asked me to take you and you knew what that meant. I know you want me physically. Aren't you satisfied with the offer?"

"You're right, Stephen. I do want you, physically. I've never quite forgotten the first time I made love and you were the lover. I guess every woman fantasizes about the first time. Maybe men do, too. But you were my fantasy, that's all you ever were. Somewhere in the back of my mind, I thought I'd show Will, get even with him for letting me down. Oh, I don't want to lie to you, Stephen, I did want you, maybe I'll always want you. And for a moment, I even considered making love with you."

Stephen stared at her. "I don't understand, Libby. I want you. I'll even consider marriage, if that's what it will take to keep you."

"No, Stephen. Someone once told me that a dream was a wonderful thing to carry around until you're face to face with the reality of it. You know who I was really seeing? It was my idea of you. The handsome, attentive man who was everything Will wasn't."

"Then stay."

"I could do that, Stephen, make love to you, become your personal assistant and leave my husband. Or, I could make love to you and go home to Will, and he'd probably never know what I'd done. But I won't do that. You know, as old-fashioned as it seems, I love Will Spencer and he's what I really want, or at least he will be when he and I sit down and really talk about it."

"Don't you think you're over-reacting, Libby? Taking this all a little too seriously? We're all what we are. Will isn't going to change. You need to see the world as it really is."

"There are a lot of things I haven't seen lately, Stephen, but I'm beginning to. Coming here with you almost made me do something very wrong for me, and I've never been more serious in my life." She'd slipped her feet in shoes she didn't even remember removing and looked around for her purse. She'd dropped it by the clothes.

"You've managed to turn my life upside down, one way or another, Stephen, and in a strange kind of way I thank you."

He made a motion to follow her and she lifted her hand to stop him. "No, stay here. I'll get home, alone. For once, Libby Spencer knows where she's going and she's wasted too much time already."

"I'm going to drive you, Libby. It's New Year's Eve and you are not going to find a cab. You don't even have a coat." He draped his jacket around her and turned out the bedroom light and followed her back to his car.

"Fine," Libby agreed finally. Flouncing out into

the night was both juvenile and impractical and suddenly she wanted to hurry, to get back to Will before midnight. Somehow, if she could get to Will before the New Year started, she'd be able to make everything right.

Impatient to get home, Libby gave Stephen directions to her apartment.

"Believe it or not, Libby," Stephen said, as they came to a stop before her apartment. "I really care for you and the last thing I want to do is cause you grief. I don't know who sent you the roses you thought came from me. I'm not a sentimental person, at least I never have been, except about you."

"I think I've figured out where the roses came from," Libby answered. "It was part of one of Dixie's foolish ideas. I should have seen it at the time. Don't worry, it wasn't your fault that I made the mistake, Stephen. You were there both times in my life when I thought I needed you. Both times I had run away from a problem I should have stayed and solved. You weren't in the wrong place, I was. Goodnight."

Libby started up the steps, stopped and flung back his jacket, calling out. "Oh, by the way, tell First Windsor Trust that Libby Spencer quits. I'm not cut out for the executive offices, it's much too perilous at the top."

Libby didn't feel the cold as she flew inside. The frozen white crystal that fell on her cheek melted into a teardrop spot of moisture. It was snowing—the scene on the Christmas cards was about to become real and she didn't even stop to watch.

Slipping off her rhinestone heels, Libby climbed

the steps two at a time. What she would find or what Will would say she didn't know. Suppose he wasn't there? Suppose he didn't understand that she'd finally grown up?

The light on the table by the door was turned on low. There was a New Year's Eve party on the TV. She walked around the couch. Will was sitting on the floor, in front of the fireplace, leaning back against the couch, a half-empty bottle of champagne on the floor beside him. He was still partially dressed in the now wrinkled black tux. The jacket and vest were thrown on the chair and his shoes and socks were clear across the room. He was here, sound asleep, celebrating the birth of a new year alone.

A ripple of *déjà vu* feathered her memory. It's happening again, she thought, like a second chance. She flew to the bedroom, stripped off all her clothes and squirted a liberal amount of perfume across her nude body. She pulled off the satin comforter, stripped the pillows from the bed, and dragged them back to the living room.

Picking up the silver tray holding the champagne and the glasses, she moved them out of reach. Carefully, she unbuttoned Will's shirt and unzipped his pants. He slipped limply into her arms, just as he had done the last time he'd passed out in her living room six years ago. Libby placed the pillows on the floor, lifted Will around on his side, sliding the pants down his lanky frame as he turned. He made a deep sigh and stretched, frightening Libby into stillness until she heard the deep, even breathing again. She caught the trouser legs and finished removing them, catching her breath as she did.

"Will Spencer, you naughty boy, you're wearing black bikini underwear, and they definitely didn't come with the tux. What did you have planned for this evening anyway?"

Suddenly, Libby felt very good as she turned out the lamp, snuggled up close to Will, and pulled the comforter over them. Just maybe, if her guardian angel was watching over her, this night would be the same as the first time and she'd have another chance with her husband. Libby sighed and reached out her hand cautiously.

Will's arm suddenly slid behind her neck and clamped her to him, while his other hand reached across her to her breast with an urgency that made Libby gasp in surprise. She could feel the full wiry length of his slim body as his arms pulled her to him. Lips descended over hers, parting them gently, tasting, seeking a wild sweet satisfaction that quickly brought a low incoherent sound from somewhere in the back of her throat. The kiss ended as he shifted her weight so that she was lying across him, looking down into lazy half-open eyes.

"Will, you're not passed out," she managed to say.

"Nope," he nuzzled her neck, sweeping his head to claim her lips once more, then released her with a grin, "and, I'll tell you a little secret, Katherine Elizabeth McHanie Spencer, my sexy, passionate, scheming wife, I wasn't passed out the first time either."

ELEVEN

Libby clutched his shoulders as she felt the wild beat of his heart, responding hungrily. Somewhere in the back of her mind she heard his words echo, but the feel of his hands now cupping the round pads of her rear, lifting her up into the hard grinding of his hips closed out everything but the electrifying tingle of her body as he kissed her.

Will released her and turned her on her back, placing her head once more on the pillow. All she heard was the pounding of her own heart and the harsh sound of Will's breath.

Will studied her. His face was confident as he recognized the physical signs of her desire, recognized and understood the dawning of knowledge in her eyes.

"What do you mean, you weren't the first time either?" Libby demanded, breathlessly, locking her fingers in Will's hair, holding him above her. "Do you mean you lay there that night, all night long, knowing that I was going crazy, and didn't make love to me?''

Libby tried to bring that night back to mind, remember all that had happened, but all she could think about now, when her body was clamoring so for attention, was that Will hadn't said anything the next morning. His fingertips were lightly circling her breasts, first one, then the other, drawing little ocean-shaped waves around her nipples.

''Yep.''

''You didn't touch me, then when I told you that you already had, you . . . Why, Will?''

''That was the worst and best night of my life,'' Will said hoarsely, leaning now to draw the same little waves around the nipples with his lips, delighting in the way she leaned toward him.

''It was?'' Will was actually talking to her, admitting the truth. She shivered, both from the intensity of the feelings he was creating and the knowledge that Will was sharing something precious with her—his thoughts.

Will smiled, capturing her lips again for a second, then pulling back. ''And I'll tell you now, that once you finally went to sleep, there wasn't an inch of your body that I didn't touch. I'll bet you had pornographic dreams that night. I did and I was wide awake.''

''And that's why, when I woke you up the next morning I was so, so aroused that I practically raped you. You must have thought I was some kind of sex maniac.'' She felt his hands moving lower, exploring now, boldly, openly. This man was not the same Will who had loved her that night.

"Sex maniac? No, ma'am. Excited? Yes. By that time, after my own stimulating night, when you let me love you it was so fantastic that I forgot *I* didn't know what to do."

His hands were circling her hips now, examining minutely her navel, touching her as though she was some new medical instrument he was unfamiliar with. This was a new Will Spencer, in charge, aggressive, and maddeningly efficient and her body began to move against him impatiently. Each time she reached the brink of no return, he paused and waited, then began to tantalize her once more.

"Oh, Will," she gasped, "you mean I was the first for you? I never knew."

"You were the first, and the only one, Libby. Then, or since, but it's never been like this for us before."

"No. Only in my fantasies," she whispered, more to herself than to him.

"And I think we should drink a toast to that." Will rolled away and retrieved the bottle of champagne.

"We're going to drink a toast, now?" Libby's voice wavered in disbelief as Will dropped back down beside her.

"Not we, me." He opened the bottle and lifted it over Libby's stomach, pouring the icy liquid into her navel, then he sat the bottle aside.

"What are you doing, you idiot?"

"Doing research, testing out a theory I had recently. It's a kind of exercise in making love." He smiled and began lapping up the cold liquid following each trail that spilled over and ran down her body, first to the side and down into the fluff of fawn-colored hair below. His rough tongue teased and caressed and drove her wild with desire.

This couldn't be Will, not the Will Spencer she'd slept with, made love with, fantasized about for most of her life. This man was some exciting creature created out of her imagination, a creature whose actions made those fantasies real. Feverishly now, a torturous heat uncoiled itself and spread over her. She arched against his mouth welcoming the darts of fire his touch ignited until she felt the rising tremble of pleasure that threatened to explode.

"Lib, oh, Lib, I'm sorry. I wanted to make it good for you, but I can't wait any longer." He swung around and plunged between her thighs to seek the molten core of heat deep within.

"Oh, oh," she moaned and pushed recklessly against him. "Will . . ."

The sound of car horns in the street, the whistles and horns on the TV signaled the end of the old year and the beginning of the new year, in a frantic roar that merged with and rode the pinnacle of their desire, exploding in a kaleidoscope of emotion.

Libby Spencer had finally found her fireworks, and pin wheels and sky rockets. She dreamed for so long about this moment. She couldn't tell whether the cry of wonder came from her or from Will or from the crowd on the television welcoming in the new year.

Will raised himself on his elbows over her. "You're a noisy wench," he chuckled, then grew more serious. "Was it . . . was it good for you, Libby?"

"Oh, Will," she whispered in languid contentment. "It was absolutely incredible." She was so overcome by the power of her emotion and the fantastic joy radiating through her body that she could hardly speak.

Will leaned down and touched her breast, teasing her nipple gently, then kissed her almost reverently before dropping back to one elbow, lining his body against her as if he too wanted to stay a part of her. His eyes crinkled in the pale light as he looked down tenderly at her and said, "By the way, Libby, I'm slow, but I'm not hopeless. I read your book in the hospital while I was sitting with Tiger, and if there's anything I'm an expert at, it's being a student."

She reached up, running the false fingernails she was still wearing down the side of his face and around his cheek bone and down his chin. "Well," she smiled, when she reached the matching thatch of fawn-colored hair brushing her leg, "I think you may have graduated with honors. I don't believe we need either book anymore." And she reached out, anxious to touch him as she'd always wanted to. She felt his sharp intake of breath and the matching response of his body, instantly rejecting its former relaxed state.

Still on his elbow, he slipped his arm under her neck, leaned down and kissed her gently. "I didn't know how to tell you how much I love you. And I was afraid you'd know that I didn't have any experience in what I was doing. I was so ignorant. I panicked and nearly lost you."

"I never knew, Will. I promise I never knew, because I didn't know what was supposed to happen to me either."

"I love you, Libby Spencer. I'm never going to

lose you again. You just have to hit me over the head now and then and bring me back to earth.'' His fingers were brushing her breast gently as though he couldn't get enough of the feel of her.

''I love you, too, Will. I've loved you all my life.'' She nuzzled the hollow of his neck as her own fingers explored and teased and learned how quickly a man's body responded to her touch.

''There's one thing I think you ought to know, Libby.''

''What?''

''I've learned a lot from Ms. Harper's book. You know what little boys do to themselves?''

''Yes. I mean, I think so. Why?''

''Well so do I. Now, I'm going to teach you what little girls do to themselves.''

''Oh, Will,'' Libby blushed, drawing back in embarrassment. ''Why do I need to know that now, when I've just learned how wonderful this is?''

''Because, beautiful lady, there may be a time tomorrow when I'm involved and I don't ever want you to be frustrated, I think you called it, not anymore.''

''Let's save something for later,'' Libby whispered, ''Right now, I'd rather practice this a little more.''

''Not yet,'' Will drew away. ''I have more to say.''

''No, Will, don't say anything to spoil this, not now.''

''Nothing can spoil this, Libby. I just want to say that even when I'm off in never, never land, I take you with me. It's as if you're there, by my side. In my imagination you always smile when I'm on the right track and you always shake your head that way you do when you're really angry with me and I know I'm wrong."

"I never knew you thought of me at all, Will, I . . ."

"That's part of the problem. We've never really talked. Neither of us ever put it into words. You were afraid not to be the perfect wife and I didn't know how to tell you what I felt. I wanted you to be honest, but I was afraid to let you."

"Oh, Will," Libby sighed, pressing herself closer. "We were such dummies."

"I know. I didn't realize that you didn't know how I felt. My folks never talked about their feelings, everybody just knew, and I guess I thought you would, too. But I'm saying it now. You're what makes my world go round, Libby. You're the dream that brings promise to my failures."

"Will, that's beautiful. I've been such a silly jealous fool. I love you so much and I almost ruined it."

"No," Will interrupted. "Let me finish. About the party. I'm so sorry." He reached down, now touching the outline of her lips with his fingertips, so softly that she almost didn't feel his touch at all. "The Tiger woke up scared and they couldn't get him quiet. I'd left word if that happened, they were to call me. I knew it would, it was just my way of getting out of part of the evening."

"It doesn't matter." Nothing mattered after what had just happened between the two of them. Libby's fingers played over Will, stroking, touching, reveling in the pulsating motion she was causing with her actions. She snuggled across him, kissing the salty taste from his chest.

"Libby," Will's voice came out in strained little spurts as though he was holding his breath. "If you don't stop what you're doing, you're going to find out firsthand what happens when little girls do to little boys what little boys do to themselves." He grabbed her hand and lifted it quickly away.

"Let me finish, now while I still have enough sense to get it all out. I almost let you down, and those kids who need experimental limbs, too. I used Tiger to stay away. Then, while I was at the hospital waiting, I went to the car and picked up your book by mistake. I began to read. Then a lot of things began to come clear. I can't believe what a fool I've been. I didn't know until then that—it's still hard to talk about this, Lib."

"Then don't."

"No, I want to say it all. I never knew until then that you'd never reached a climax. I've been a lousy lover. Once I figured that out, I went to the party to tell you."

"Oh?" Libby held her breath. What was coming next? Was everything to end just when she'd learned what it was she'd been looking desperately for?

"You went to the party?"

"Yes, and I was wrong about Dixie and her friends. Bill Pullen and the university will be amazed at the money donated. Those people were really interested in what I'm doing."

Dixie, the party. Libby's heart almost stopped. "Did Dixie tell you where I went?"

"No," Will said softly. "She just sent me home, said you'd be along, and she said another strange thing—I was to tell you that she was wrong, love is for tomorrow, yesterday, and forever."

"Will, I need to tell you . . ."

"No," he said, sealing her lips. "New Year's resolutions. No looking back. We have a brand new year to start over in, and," he kissed her again, "you know, tomorrow has already started."

"Will, no matter what you say, I think I'd better tell you one thing. I've quit my job."

"Mummm, I think I'd better tell you that I already have another one in mind for you."

"So do I. You hear mine first." She tried not to feel the rising desire beginning to make her body move unevenly.

He slid down until his body was side by side with hers, totally meshed with hers and the tips of her nipples touched his chest every time she breathed.

"Oh, Will, I . . ."

"You were going to tell me about your new job, dear."

"I thought, as old-fashioned as it sounds, I might apply for full-time motherhood, if you don't mind, and I could do some volunteer work on the side."

"Libby," Will gasped as Libby, unable to lie without touching him, reached out once more and ran her fingers lightly across his chest, leaving a rippling path as her hand was drawn into the thick, wiry hair below.

"That's exactly the kind of project I had in mind," he whispered. "I see you've been reading the same manuals as me. I definitely approve of your technical approach.''

"But I haven't proved my hypothesis,'' she whispered. "I'm still deciding where I want to put in my job application.''

"Oh, right here. You're certainly making the best choice. But you know I'm going to have to check your references, very carefully.'' And Will Spencer proceeded to do just that.

"I must say this is the nicest interview I've ever had,'' Libby smiled happily. "If every potential employer used your technique, we might end unemployment.''

"I may have missed my calling. Perhaps I ought to change to personnel.''

"I expect you'd better tell me what you think about my qualifications, Will. I don't believe I can wait to complete my application much longer.''

"Let's just say,'' he answered quickly, "if the job works out, your progress may not be up,'' he patted her stomach tenderly, following his hands with a kiss, "but it most assuredly will be out.''

"I accept the offer. Could we begin right now?'' She reached eagerly for him, her hands pulling him frantically to her.

"Throw away the pills?''

"I already did,'' she grinned. "And, I warn you, I expect an iron-clad, no-trade employment contract.''

"Granted, providing you call a board of directors meeting the next time you think we aren't communicating. I think you're right about the book.''

"What book?'' she asked breathlessly, thrusting her body against him.

"Angel Harper's *Secrets to a More Exciting Sex Life*, I don't think we need it anymore."

"Oh? Think you learned it all, do you?"

"No," he groaned, not allowing himself to enter her, not yet, content to rest his body on top, feeling the excitement of her torment beneath him. "No, I don't think I've learned it all, but I'm getting there." And, touching his lips to her nose, he proceeded to review the material and Libby followed him willingly through every chapter.

"Somehow, I don't think this kind of instruction was in the book I read," she gasped.

"Oh, I don't know," Will whispered, rakishly. "You talk too much."

He was patient this time, content to hold his own passion in tight control. The glazed, heavy look of desire in her eyes had to be a reflection of his own. A sense of wonder swept over him as he came to know the exquisite joy of total abandonment from this woman he'd lived with almost as a stranger.

Slowly and carefully he held back, bringing her along gently, as he would the discovery of a precious new creation in his lab. Suddenly she arched against him, a rippling of powerful release swept over both of them and her cry of passion was the most satisfying prize he'd ever known as a man.

Tenderly, he pressed his lips against hers and knew that she'd touched his soul.

"Do you hear it?" Libby asked much later, lying in contented languor as she listened to Will talk about his work.

"Hear what?"

"Something on the roof?"

"Well, it can't be Santa unless he's taking the long way home. The new year has already come and gone. And it's too early for the stork."

"Maybe," Libby agreed, "it's probably the snow. When we get up the ground will be covered and we won't be able to get out of the apartment."

"That's fine with me," Will agreed, curving his body to hers and pulling up the comforter. "I kinda like it right where I am."

"So do I."

Libby felt very warm and very good and perhaps she was almost asleep when Will said something under his breath. "There is it again, Lib, the sound, like feathers brushing against the roof."

"Silly, Will," Libby whispered, "don't you know? That's the sound of angel wings."

EPILOGUE

Will would probably be late. Libby had long ago accepted that. He never meant to be, but some little detail would catch his attention and an hour later he'd look up and realize that dinner was long over, or the movie had already started. Then he'd call and rush home, pushing his green truck to the protesting point.

Libby pressed her hand against her lower back and groaned. She ought to be angry, but she wasn't. She only had to recall that Will now had the same fascination with her body, discovering some new response, some new feeling of wonder that he'd never elicited before.

More mornings than not he was as late to work as he was arriving home. She figured that it all evened itself out. Besides, perfection had never been her goal. Loving Will was, and being loved in return.

The nagging back pain had started right after Will left for work this morning and it had grown steadily.

The obstetrician had warned her that carrying two babies was a strain on her slight figure.

"Bend your knees," he'd suggested, "and change your position. Lying on your side would relieve the pressure."

But this morning nothing helped. With over three weeks to go before her delivery date, Libby refused to even look in the mirror. She looked like a watermelon. And her breasts—Will might be telling the truth when he expressed his appreciation at their new proportions, but he didn't have to carry them around.

It was hard to believe that only a year ago she'd been certain that if her breasts were bigger Will would be interested in her. It hadn't been the size of her breasts that had changed their marriage, nor had it been the love that had always been there.

Libby lumbered to her feet and plodded into the bedroom. Tucked between the pages of a book were two pictures. One likeness was that of a small boy, standing in front of a pink castle with Mickey Mouse on one side and Minnie on the other. He looked like a smiley face with two arms, two arms holding up his hands in a boxer's gesture of success.

They'd made the picture on their trip to the amusement park the week before Tiger had returned to his own country and his real family. But he'd be back. Will had promised that there would always be a place for Tiger in their home and in their hearts.

The second picture was a color shot that made the cover of the magazine section of the newspaper. Stephen Colter, the new financial genius who'd been tapped by the Olympic Committee to handle the financial planning of the Summer Olympics of 1996, which were being held in Atlanta. First Windsor, the new kid on the local banking block, fighting bad press over discontinued services, had graciously agreed to pay Stephen's salary and expenses while he handled the Olympic event.

Blue eyes stared out at Libby from the picture as if Stephen had been sending a message straight to her. He had cared about her. But they'd been two ships that passed in the night, each offering something the other needed at that time in their lives, and moving on when the need was met. Libby smiled. A little part of her would always care about Stephen, but that was all right. Life was made up of all that was good, and bad, and the challenge was to deal with each. In the end, a person grew with every new challenge.

Grew? Libby glanced down at her stomach. Maybe this was overdoing the growth process a bit. Libby smiled and closed the book. She wandered over to the window and pulled back the drape. Darkness had already fallen. Through the fine rain shimmering in the blackness, she looked beyond the neat front yard of their house, beyond the wrought-iron fence that ran around it like finishing stitches on the crib blankets she'd been making. She could see the streetlight wearing a halo in the icy mist.

Addie Spencer's words had been right. The babies came with the love, not with the license. But when she'd wished for a child, she never expected such generosity. Though she should have. Will had never done anything halfway in his life. Not his schooling, not his job, and not loving her. It was simply a matter of concentration.

They'd cried when they released Tiger to the woman who was taking him back to his country. They'd missed him and Will had reminded her of their plan to have a child of their own.

For the first time since they'd married, Will turned his attention to her with the same amount of persistence and vigor he'd shown in catching frogs in the creek behind their house. With Will's unique mind and ability to study his subject, making love was considerably much more interesting than catching frogs.

Still, making a baby hadn't happened instantly. Almost four months went by. Just when she was beginning to worry, she learned that she was pregnant. The pregnancy worked out perfectly with the closing of her branch bank, and with Stephen Colter's being made CEO of the Atlanta branches of Windsor Trust.

Libby checked the kitchen clock again and glanced back at the street. Will was later than usual. Normally, she didn't mind. When he came in, he was full of information about his work and he was more than willing to share Libby's day, finding pleasure in even the smallest thing.

It wasn't what they were doing that interested the other, it was that they were sharing the doing of it.

But tonight she felt a tinge of worry. The weather was growing more treacherous by the minute and Will wasn't the most attentive driver in the world. At least he had learned not to misplace his truck, or maybe Pat had learned to watch out for his friend.

The roast was done, still warm in the oven. Tiny onions and new potatoes and green beans filled the casserole dish in the microwave, ready to be heated. Miss Lois and her friends had insisted on caring for Libby, sending little dishes and sweets by way of Lewis Marvin on a regular basis when he went by to run their errands and handle their money now that Libby was at the end of her pregnancy.

A quick, sharp pain sliced through Libby's thoughts, unexpectedly attacking her back, and she couldn't hold back a cry. What was happening? She held her breath and waited for the pain to pass before straightening up. Then it was gone and she breathed again.

She couldn't be going into labor. Libby Spencer did things on schedule and the time wasn't right yet. Resolutely, she put the thought out of her mind. "It's snowing," she said with wonder in her voice. "No," she corrected her observation as she leaned her forehead against the cold pane and let out her breath, "it's sleeting." The fine white particles streaked the darkness, blurring as her breath fogged the window.

The pain was gone but there was still a heaviness that bothered her. Probably only one of the babies was pinching a nerve or pressing against her spinal cord. Whatever it was, it was gone now. Libby checked her watch: seven o'clock. "Will Spencer, you'd better get home or the roads are going to be icy!"

But Will didn't come. When another hour passed, Libby began to worry. The pain came back sharply, in quick little jabs that cut with fierce determination, then vanished, leaving her convinced that she'd imagined them.

Outside, the smears of white became freezing rain mixed with lacy flakes of snow. It was sticking to the trees and lawn like glaze on a sugar cake. Libby could hear the occasional crash of a limb, breaking under the weight of the ice and falling to the ground. Maybe she ought to call the doctor and warn him. She didn't think that she could possibly be in labor, but it wouldn't hurt to check in.

The phone was dead. Libby allowed a moment of panic to sweep over her. She felt as if she were in some blank void as she stood with the receiver pressed against her ear, listening to the singing emptiness.

The next pain that came wasn't short and it wasn't a mistake. She doubled up and cried out as she felt the sudden gush of wetness cascade down the inside of her legs in hot confirmation. She was definitely in labor.

She'd have to drive herself. Libby waited for the pain to pass, then waddled to the bathroom to clean herself. Another pain shot through her and she cried out. The pressure that accompanied the pain told her that the hospital was going to be too far. She'd never make it. Her babies were coming now, and she was all alone.

"Damn you, Will Spencer," Libby swore, then regretted her words. Their babies weren't supposed to come yet. The phone wasn't supposed to be out. That wasn't Will's fault. She grabbed an armful of towels and made her way to the bed. With the last of her strength, she slid her clothes from her body and fell into the bed.

"Will. Will, please, I need you! Come home, Will."

*   *   *

Will looked up from the computer and went very still. He was alone. Everybody else had gone. When? He hadn't even heard them leave. Glancing across at the window, he groaned. The pane was streaked with ice and the lights flickered ominously on and off. What was happening?

Then he heard it, as clearly as if Libby were standing behind him. "Will, Will, I need you."

In a clatter of falling papers and books, Will came to his feet, grabbed his coat, and dashed out of his office and down the hall. His truck was the only one left in the parking deck, a deck that was more like a skating rink than a parking area.

Under the best of conditions Will's driving was much like his life—erratic, undisciplined, and wild. This trip home would test the skill of the winner of the Indy 500. Will knew he was in big trouble.

How had he let the time get away from him? With Libby eight-months pregnant, he ought not to be taking any chances. She was at home alone, probably madder than a hen whose eggs had been tampered with. Libby, even saying her name brought a calming effect to his breathing. The last year had been so perfect that he felt as if he was living in a dream, afraid that he'd wake up any minute and she'd be gone.

Libby, he'd almost lost her. Libby, the steady balance in his life. Libby, whose touch set him on fire and carried him to heights of physical pleasure that he'd never dreamed of. He'd never told her that Stephen Colter had come to see him, had asked him to release Libby. Colter accused him of not appreciating Libby's loyalty and said that he thought the two of them were more suited. Will had been stunned. He refused to agree. He'd never let Libby go. He didn't blame Colter. He didn't blame Libby. It had been his own insensitivity that made Libby reach out to Stephen. But Libby loved Will Spencer. She always had.

Three months ago he'd met Stephen at a Chamber of Commerce function. He'd forced himself to speak to the man, shaking his hand. "Colter, I know how close I came to losing Libby. I just wanted to say, thanks. I don't even mind your sending her flowers."

"I never sent her flowers, Spencer," he'd said, "though perhaps I should have. Besides, the truth is, I'd have taken her, if I could. I couldn't. Libby Spencer is a very special lady."

It had been Dixie who sent the flowers. Will had been wrong in not believing her. Will had been wrong about a lot of things. He felt the tires slide and he swore. "Not now, please, if there's anybody up there that can hear me, don't let anything happen now. Libby needs me!

"And God, I need her!"

The truck straightened itself and, as if it had wings, it raced along the deserted streets until the house came into view. He didn't make it up the drive. The truck skidded across the drive, crashing into the gate. That was close enough. Slipping and sliding he made his way across the lawn and into the house.

"Libby! Where are you?"

"Will?"

She was in the bedroom, holding her stomach and

panting in those quick, shallow breaths they'd practiced.

"Libby, you're not—"

"I'm in labor, Will."

"I'll call an ambulance."

"The phone's out."

"Then I'll drive you. Damn! The truck's blocking the drive."

"Willllllll!" Libby caught her lower lip between her teeth and swallowed his name. "It's too late, Will. I think our babies are about to be born."

"But, Libby—what shall I do?"

Even in her pain Libby laughed. Her wonderfully, inept husband was asking her what to do. "Will, you're a doctor. Get your doctor's bag and deliver your children."

"A doctor, yes. I do have a bag, someplace. Of course." As if a light had been switched on, Will straightened his shoulders, concentrated on remembering where he'd put his medical supplies, and turned to the task at hand.

The first baby was a boy, all arms and legs, squalling his displeasure at being forced into the world. Will cleaned his eyes, tied off the cord, and laid him on Libby's stomach. Libby slid him forward, her eyes filled with love as he nuzzled her nipple and clasped it greedily.

"Just like his father," she said.

"A wise boy," Will agreed and turned to the task of readying Libby for the next birth.

Their daughter was born twenty minutes later. She was pink and soft and wide-eyed. Will held her perfect little body in his arms and felt a surge of love wash over him. Tears ran unashamedly down his cheeks and he marveled at the wonder of what he'd experienced.

Hours later, an exhausted but happy Libby lay in Will's arms. The babies slept between them. Outside, the sleet and snow continued to fall. But Will and Libby were cushioned by a cocoon of love that kept them warm and safe.

"How did you get here, Will?"

"I heard you call me."

"I don't understand."

"Neither do I. But I knew that you needed me and I came."

"But the roads. Nobody has passed, not even a police car. How?"

"I—" he hesitated, trying to put something unexplainable into words, "I honestly don't know, Libby. There were times when I felt like the truck left the ground, as if I was flying."

"Knowing how you drive I can believe that."

"No, it was as if the truck had wings."

Wings. Then he remembered what had been nagging at the fringes of his mind for most of the night. He'd sensed that once before, when Libby had come back to him that New Year's Eve. It had been snowing then. And that swishing sound on the roof, he'd quipped that it couldn't be Santa Claus.

"Well, whatever got you here, I'm grateful, Will. I needed you and you came. I don't ever want to be apart from you."

"Nor I, Libby. What shall we name them?" Will

reached across the sleeping babies and caught Libby's hand, as if that connection sealed their commitment.

"Don't laugh, Will, but I thought we'd name our son Gabriel."

"Gabriel? Of course. That's what it should be."

"But what about our daughter?" Libby asked, snuggling closer so that her head could rest on Will's shoulder.

"Elizabeth, of course. Gabriel and Elizabeth."

"But you already have one Elizabeth—me."

"Now I have two. Oh, Libby, darling. You've made me so very happy. I wish we could—I mean I wish I could show you. Damn, what am I saying. You've just had two babies."

"Will," she said shyly. "I wish you could, too. It won't be long."

Long after Libby slept, Will stood beside the bed standing guard over his wife and his children. Tomorrow Libby would go to the hospital where they'd check out the babies and make certain that they were all right.

But for now they were his, his wife and his family. And he knew such joy as he'd never known. When the sun rose the next morning, he walked to the bedroom window and stared at the ground below. In the unmarred surface of the snow below there were two strange indentions.

"What is that, Will?" Libby asked as she slid her arm around his waist and looked down at the lawn.

"Didn't you ever play in the snow as a child?"

"No, and neither did you. Why?"

"Then we'll learn to do that together. What you

do is lie down in the snow and move your arms up and down, as if you're flying.''

"Oh," she said, allowing her lips to widen into a happy smile as Will moved behind her and slid his arms around her. "Oh, yes, Will, I see them—angel wings.''

SHARE THE FUN . . .
SHARE YOUR NEW-FOUND TREASURE!!

You don't want to let your new books out of your sight? That's okay. Your friends can get their own. Order below.

No. 37 ROSES by Caitlin Randall
It's an inside job & K.C. helps Brett find more than the thief!

No. 38 HEARTS COLLIDE by Ann Patrick
Matthew finds big trouble and it's spelled P-a-u-l-a.

No. 39 QUINN'S INHERITANCE by Judi Lind
Gabe and Quinn share an inheritance and find an even greater fortune.

No. 40 CATCH A RISING STAR by Laura Phillips
Justin is seeking fame; Beth helps him find something more important.

No. 41 SPIDER'S WEB by Allie Jordan
Silvia's quiet life explodes when Fletcher shows up on her doorstep.

No. 42 TRUE COLORS by Dixie DuBois
Julian helps Nikki find herself again but will she have room for him?

No. 43 DUET by Patricia Collinge
Adam & Marina fit together like two perfect parts of a puzzle!

No. 44 DEADLY COINCIDENCE by Denise Richards
J.D.'s instincts tell him he's not wrong; Laurie's heart says trust him.
